Wall to Wall

Michael Pennington (Deceased)

First published in Great Britain
Pen Press Publishers Ltd
39-41 North Road
London N7 9DP

ISBN 1-904754-62-7

A catalogue record for this book is available
from the British Library

Printed and bound in Great Britain

Cover design by Jacqueline Abromeit

*Dedicated to the numerous contributors
and thousands of guests on the original
Message Forum that made this story
possible.*

Preface

My Dear friends, I am about to take you on a wonderful journey that begins in the city of Birmingham, England. What I am about to reveal will challenge your mind and stretch the boundaries of your imagination, on subjects that have been of great controversy and intrigue since time immemorial. Whether or not you choose to believe or disbelieve is of little relevance with regard to my mission. This publication is the result of an amazing story that has found its way to all corners of the globe. From humble beginnings on a web site in Birmingham, our mission is being replicated across the internet and in many message forums and chat rooms around the world.

Introduction

My name is Michael Pennington. I have lived in a very old property in Oldbury for a number of years now. It is by a canal and has been in a dilapidated state for over thirty years, having once been used as a repair boatyard for those using the canals.

However, very recently the building has been converted to an office. The transformation is amazing – builders have restored the old beams, the roof no longer leaks, the painters and decorators have done a wonderful job on the interior and this is now a very desirable residence in which to live.

I originally had no experience of computers but I listened to the office workers every day and I would watch them intensely on occasions. I really had no idea that I would one day be able to operate a computer. I am amazed at what has happened and how I have managed to master and understand the operation of computers and the internet. Technology is a wonderful thing. My computer experience has changed my very existence. It started around Christmas time but I had better give you a little background information first. My story goes back some time…

A New Beginning

In March 1971 I was walking along the canal bank. New attempts were being made to turn the canals into leisure areas and this particular walkway was in good order. It was a typical spring day around 2 p.m. in the afternoon, the weather was bright and sunny. The spring breeze blew gently against the trees which swayed to and fro against the bright blue sky. The weather had been dry for some time and the wind created twirls of dust which spiralled into the air from the canal walkway.

I had just been promoted at the textile firm which I had worked for since leaving school. From humble beginnings on the shop floor, I had risen through the ranks to the position of manager. Life was good and I was married with a wonderful daughter named Geraldine. We had just purchased our first house and we were looking forward to our first family holiday abroad. I considered myself fortunate and prided myself on the fact that my hard work and dedication over the years had finally paid off.

I was nearing my place of work and I had just passed the doorway of this old boatyard building, the very same one in which I now live. Suddenly someone grabbed me from behind and I could hear agitated voices and felt a sharp pain in my back. What followed was something I would not wish on anyone. Essentially I was beaten to a pulp and thrown down the coal shaft of this particular property.

To this day I have no idea why they did this to me but it has affected me ever since and it is one of the reasons why I have these psychic powers. Birmingham is a busy place so I waited for someone to pass the building so that I could shout and attract someone's attention. I was feeling weak and miserable and in considerable pain. I drifted in and out of sleep for some time. I could feel that I was sitting in a pool of my own blood. I was desperate to get out of there as the weather was getting colder and colder. What happened next was really strange and beyond all comprehension.

I think it was morning time when I found myself looking down on my own body. I nearly had a heart attack but realised that for something like that to happen I would have to be actually present in my own body. There was a pool of blood around my lifeless figure. I looked stony cold and strange. It gave me the shudders. I could see that I had been pushed down a deep shaft. I really did look a mess. I observed with horror the extent of the beatings I had taken and could hardly recognise myself.

Nervously inching forward I tried to find a way to climb out of the room I was in. I could see the light coming in from the doors that I had been bundled through. They were about twice my height in distance from the uneven floor of the poorly lit room. Only a ray of sunlight provided the means by which to see and I could not fully comprehend the extent of the size of the room or make out the far wall. At this point I realised that the wall had a rubbery sensation. The ground had that same creepy feeling to it. In fact, I found that I could not actually touch anything properly. It was then that I became paranoid. This was not an out-of-body experience at all. I had actually died. I was dead. No more me. But why was I thinking? Why was I even able to see my own lifeless corpse on the ground. Was I a ghost? I cannot begin to express the strange feelings and the sense of awe and fear that I had at the time. If I was a spirit, then what on earth was my purpose? What are ghosts supposed to do and was I destined to spend an eternity in this dingy trap that had suddenly become my prison? I had no explanation. There was no logic or reason.

I hate to admit it – I cried. I did all the usual feeling sorry for myself, thinking about what relatives and friends might be wondering. How would they find me? Would they ever find me? Was my will up to date? It is difficult to explain the wide range of feelings that goes through one's mind when faced with such a terrifying experience. I constantly thought about my wife and daughter and how things had changed so suddenly and without any rational explanation. My situation was so desperate, and caused so much anguish, that had I been alive I would surely have contemplated suicide. Such was the extent of my feelings and the helpless situation I now found myself in.

The first few days were the worst. Stuck there, nothing happening, no hope, no visitors, no nothing. It was on the fifth day that the light was particularly strong and I could make out a staircase towards the far end of the room. I had not ventured anywhere where I could not see. Crazy as it may sound I am scared of the dark and I was worried about venturing into the dark unknown. As if I wasn't already there.

When I reached the staircase it had the same rubbery spongy feeling as the walls and floor but I could move up it. I could actually tread each step and move upwards. I remember thinking at the time that this was a ridiculous situation to be in. I mean, ghosts are supposed to walk through walls are they not? Imagine my absolute sense of joy when I found that I was on another floor and could walk round five rooms, with offices and a repair yard. Then the sense of elation that I had when I discovered yet another floor with more rooms and an area that had been used as living accommodation. You might think it strange that I was so excited, but how would you have liked to have remained in that dark dungeon below?

Time passed by. Each day was pretty much the same as the last. I memorised every object in the building and would sit for hours and hours watching people from the window as they passed by the canal walkway. No one ever found my body. I never ventured down there again. It depressed me, the thought of what had been me, slowly decaying in that dank and dark room. Gradually over a period of time I was buried under rubbish and waste that people kept throwing in through the open shaft. Some years back the foundations of the building were shored up and concrete was poured into the room via a long tube from a barge, carrying what must have been ready-mixed concrete. I suppose it was in an effort to stop the building becoming unstable. This property was built around the 1850s.

My life, or lack of life, became a routine. I would always wonder why I was in this situation. If this happened to everyone then why didn't I see other spirits or ghosts? Why couldn't I walk through walls or windows and get outside?

I had a burning desire and an ambition to explore the great outdoors and yet I was trapped and unable to find a way out of my prison. I craved for some company and longed for the sound of human voices once again. Being alone with all my thoughts was the worst part of it all, and the fact that I could not touch or move anything was depressing. I had an old newspaper sitting on the floor for years and could only read the pages that were open. Over and over again I read it until it faded with time and became unreadable.

There are many thoughts that occur when faced with such a lifeless and futile existence. I would happily have exchanged my fate for a prison cell or worse, as at least I would have had some company and the comfort of being able to confide and interact with a living soul. I was so bitter and resentful, it is amazing that I managed to retain my sanity over those long and destitute years that seemed like an eternity.

No one ever came. I was so lonely. For years no one paid any attention to the building at all. I do not really know how long it was before the first visitor came. That was an experience I can tell you. It was a rainy day and the two well dressed gentlemen turned up in one of those fancy new cars (cars were getting more and more modern and the skyline had changed dramatically) with what I imagine was someone from the Council and a surveyor. I listened with excitement to the clunking and battering of the door which continued for several minutes as they struggled to gain entry. All of a sudden the door burst open and I was face to face with the first real people I had seen close up in years. It's no good asking me how many years because time had no meaning for me. Well, not until recently.

Here I was, face to face with real live people again and what did I do? I made a bolt for the open door. I remember the trauma of it all. The open space that they had just walked through was for me that same rubbery touch and feel of the walls, the floor and everything else. My heart, or perhaps I should say my spirit, sank. No escape for me after all these years.

Still, I was going to make the most of this. I could clearly hear them talking as if I was actually alive. They were surveying the building. New development was mentioned. Demolition or conversion was discussed. I leapt up and down, screamed at them, tried to push them, anything to try and communicate. Nothing. It's awkward but when you want people to talk and talk because you miss human contact, they don't say much. I mean, this was the most exciting thing that had happened for years, and they spent most of their time with a tape measure, making notes.

The men were in their early fifties. Imagine my surprise when one of the men looked straight at me and stared in my direction with a puzzled look on his face. Seizing the opportunity I ran towards him shouting and screaming and trying to push him, staring into his eyes, pressing my face right up close against his. He had this really odd look on his face but I knew he couldn't see me. What could it be? What had made him stare towards me in that way with a distracted look and lack of concentration? He was as rubbery and non touchable as everything else and yet I could pass through him like I could a closed door. I have never worked out why I cannot walk outside through the solid walls and yet I can pass effortlessly around the interior of the building and its partitions and internal doorways. Don't believe everything you read in ghost stories. Trust me, I know.

It was then that he surprised me. He came straight out with it. I remember the words as if he had just spoken them. "Tom, this place gives me the creeps. I keep feeling as if there is someone else here with us," he said.

Can you imagine how I felt? Somehow he had managed to sense or pick up something from me. A sixth sense perhaps. I wish I could have been a poltergeist and capable of throwing something around the room, but years of trying had conditioned me to the fact that I had no control over my surroundings and no way of influencing my unfortunate circumstances. Nothing else eventful happened that day. Tom dismissed his friend's comment with a callous and flippant remark about the building possibly being haunted.

Time and seasons passed again. I had hoped that things would have improved after their visit but nothing changed. That is, until June 21st 2003. How would I know that? I will explain. One day the doors of the building burst open. My whole world was interrupted by a band of seven men charging through the building talking excitedly about materials and making lists and running hither and thither in all directions.

Things were about to change. My world became a hive of activity. A radio burst into life and I knew what year and day I was in. Over thirty years had passed. It had seemed like a thousand years. All of a sudden I was learning things again. I was taking in information, watching real live people as they started to transform my home. This was real excitement. The sound of the Brummie workmen, how I had missed that accent, how I had missed people. My world was alive. Every day was different and new people would come and go. They carried strange little plastic and metal phones that had no leads or obvious connections. I know these are mobile phones now, but imagine my surprise at the time. Many objects were foreign to me. I just had not seen them before. These days I know as much as you do. Probably more. You will see why in due course.

Within just a couple of months I was wandering around a wonderful and bright new building. It was modern and comfortable and designed in a style that was most pleasing and new to me. The lighting is so soothing and natural, and at nights I have a light now, which I never had before. They always leave a light on for me. I am so grateful for that.

Without doubt this new chapter of events has transformed my existence. I actually know that I do exist. The building work is finished, and there are twenty-one people who work from these offices. They are a consultancy firm and I know every character and name. I know what the manager gets up to after hours in his office, and I know that the cleaner is having an affair with the sales executive. The most fascinating thing of all is watching what they do on their computers. I used to watch for hours on end, day after day. I read everything that appeared on their screens. I would move from one desk to another and absorb the information feverishly.

Nothing can compensate for the loss of my humanity, but at the same time I cannot begin to explain how wonderful it was to be in the company of people once again. I hated the evenings, nights and weekends when I was alone, and would look forward to the busy office environment, and the day-to-day conversations of the workers as they went about their business.

Janet appeared on the scene one day and without warning. This was strange because I used to sit in on interviews and find out just who was starting or leaving employment with the firm. Janet must have had her interview off site and I must have missed out on any conversation about her. The thing about Janet is that she knows I am here and she is very receptive, she has a sixth sense and is not fearful of my existence. She comes from Dudley.

Janet used to comment about feeling the place was haunted when I got close to her but her office colleagues would just laugh and she soon gave up. Janet reads the news online and reads more interesting things than the others do. Janet is not as busy as the rest of the office workers and has quite a bit of spare time. She has noticed over time that whenever she is reading the news or anything of interest, she can feel my presence. At first she was nervous but is now comfortable. Imagine my surprise one day when I sat down beside her and she turned towards me and said quietly, "I know you are there, I can feel that you are around. You like the news don't you." I was overjoyed. I suddenly felt recognised and no longer alone. Janet gave me a whole new sense of perspective and hope and ambition. Janet was the one that finally taught me how to communicate with the outside world in a way I never thought possible.

There are certain considerations and concerns I have about sharing this story with you and everyone else. I mean, for obvious reasons most people are going to think that this is all an elaborate hoax. I also would hate to lead anyone down the garden path but all will be revealed. Be patient with me, I have so much more to do, so much more to tell. I am using a laptop computer from the office. Janet is communicating with me and I have proved to her that I am what I am. She is helping me to break through the boundaries of what you would probably call the supernatural.

How did I find a way to create type? How do I access the internet? What is it I want? Just what is the reason that I am here? What are ghosts supposed to do? I know you will have your theories, your guesses. Some may be right, others will be wrong. There will be surprises for you too. I am also not the only spirit mind to be using the internet. There are hundreds of us, thousands in fact.

I am at a loss to understand why I cannot be seen at all. I have hope that someone with special equipment will be able to actually see me at some point in the future. Apparently ghosts give off some form of electricity if we are to believe the claims of the professional ghost hunters. This is of course assuming that I am indeed a ghost. I will refer to myself as a ghost or a spirit. I have to accept that I am not alive. I do however exist.

Janet could only sense me initially, but that was to change as you will learn later. She still cannot see me. Prior to Janet's arrival, the only time I had actually had anyone else sense me was when I had that visit some years back from the surveyor and his colleague. This is strange in itself as there are many visitors to the office and there are twenty-one full-time workers here.

Janet has a gift in the form of a sixth sense. She is single and thirty-four years of age. I suppose Janet typifies what you might imagine a secretary or administrator of a small firm to be like. She is single and of quiet disposition. Janet is always well dressed and takes pride in her personal appearance. I suppose some would argue that Janet is very straight-laced and prim and proper. From my point of view she is one of the most wonderful and sensitive people I have ever met, dead or alive.

When they rebuilt the property here in Oldbury, they did not dig out the concrete that had been poured into the dark cellar in which I became entombed. I never go down there and whilst some of the workers did venture into the basement a few times I have no idea what work was carried out. There is no way in from the outside now, as the hole that I was pushed through has been bricked up. The door that used to lead to the cellar area is no longer there. That doorway was bricked up too. I had been sealed in my tomb.

I would constantly question my existence and struggle to understand the reason for my presence here on earth. Am I here because my body has not been found? If it is found and I have a decent burial then what happens to me afterwards? Some writings refer to the spirit being confused and not knowing how to move on. Move on where?

With regard to my skills I will elaborate on this later. I have been a quick learner. It is easy to learn quickly when you have so much time and you do not sleep at all. Time is all I have. I do not eat or drink and I am not bound by time-consuming issues that use up so many valuable resources of the living.

One day I was at Janet's side reading the latest news as she scrolled through the BBC web site. Nothing was really much different than any previous day but I could see that Janet was in deep thought. She suddenly whispered, "Let's see what we can find out about ghosts and spirits." I was so pleased that she had been inspired by my presence and that she was going to try and help me. She must have spent hours and hours surfing the internet and we read many topics and some quite cranky tales about ghosts and spirits.

Some of the information is very informative and some is just downright ridiculous. I even read that only evil folk or people who have done something wrong in life can possibly end up as ghosts. This was written by some fool in Utah in the USA. Just what does he know?

Janet was engrossed in the subject and so was I. From that day on, Janet would spend around an hour each day just on the subject of the supernatural and paranormal. There is so much information out there. She is so considerate and would even leave her laptop on at night with a news ticker, a sports ticker and anything else she could find of interest so that I would not get bored. She still does. She is also the person who made sure that a light was left on at nights. The most frustrating part of my predicament was that I could not thank her and would have to settle for her just knowing that I was there, or so I thought.

On September last, I had read all the information that was flashing up and down on the news tickers and the repetitive scrolling was beginning to become a bit tedious. I looked carefully at the keyboard of Janet's laptop and examined the machine in minute detail. Every little piece of information is so important to me. If I had my time again I would study and be as hungry for knowledge as I am now. You never appreciate these things when you are alive. I mean, I did not have anything else to do except hang around.

I was becoming acquainted with computers. After all, I watched everything and everybody here at the office. The laptop at the office is connected to a permanent internet connection. It is with BT Broadband and the company has a server. This was what brought my attention to the flashing light showing the 'wireless on' connection. Janet had somehow accidentally activated it when it wasn't necessary for a connection to the internet.

I moved my hand over the keyboard in deep thought and wished that I could operate this marvel of technology. I met with that same spongy touch and rubbery feel and I sighed as only a spirit can sigh. It was then that I noticed what I thought was a slight movement in the mouse cursor. I ran my hand over the keyboard again and willed it to do something. This time I was sure that the mouse cursor flickered. I pressed both of my hands on the laptop and pushed as I have pushed and pulled on things a thousand times in the past. To my surprise and astonishment, the internet explorer browser suddenly opened. For the first time since my death I actually felt something physical. I felt a kind of electrical charge pass through my non-existent body. I was astounded. Something phenomenal had happened here.

After hours of experimentation, and with great excitement, I found that I could place my finger, that is, place what I understand as my finger, and where my finger would have been if I was human, on the mouse pad, and move the cursor around the screen. The wireless connection indicator was flickering as if a signal was present. I was frantic with excitement and desperation. All night I moved the cursor in short jerky movements backwards and forwards across the desktop. By early morning I had mastered how to open the internet browser at will and close and open other programs on the laptop. It now occurred to me that the wireless connection might have something to do with my new found ability in being able to make the laptop function. What if Janet noticed it on and decided to turn it off. I was fighting against time. I needed to do something.

I opened a word document. Painstakingly slowly I mastered how to make a letter of the alphabet appear on the open document. It is hard to convey to you the sense of pride and achievement that I felt. For over thirty years I could only watch and observe. Suddenly something wonderful had given me the chance to do something that I had never thought possible in my wildest dreams. Ghosts do dream you know. Well, in a sense, although we are awake all the time.

I had to stop Janet from cutting off this connection. I started to try and write her a note. How could I explain? It was taking me too long, she would be coming into work soon. Each letter of the alphabet was taking me an age to write. Another astounding discovery – I had never, until now, and since my death, been concerned about time. I was acting all human again.

What if Janet treated the note as a cheap prank and ignored my message? How could I convince her that I was here and that what she had sensed was now trying to communicate with her? Imagine how you would feel. I had no choice, and no time. I wrote:

Do not turn off the wireless switch. Your friend Michael Pennington died March 19th 1971. Please please plea...

That was as far as I got. I heard her unlocking the door and turning off the alarm. She was soon at her desk. I would have held my breath but... Well you know... Janet put her handbag down beside the chair and went straight to make a coffee. This was a routine she carried out every morning. I was worried. I thought she would have seen the message straight away. When she came back she stopped in her tracks and stared at the screen. Janet had been last to lock up and was the first to open up the office. I was banking on that fact. Suddenly Janet smiled, turned, and walked back down the corridor. Something was wrong.

I followed her to the alarm control panel. Janet was checking the last recorded entry that had been made into the premises. Her face was a picture when she realised that no one but herself had been in there since the alarm was last set. Back to the computer we went. I saw her looking worried and confused. I didn't like that, but this was so important. Janet sat at her desk and stared at the message – the open word document with its message that had taken me so long to type. Was she convinced? Probably not. I did not know.

Janet started to type a message under my text on the open document:

This is ridiculous, I don't even know why I am bothering to type this, but if you are there, and I feel that I can sense something, please reply.

I had to do something fast. I concentrated, pressed into the spongy rubbery void over the keyboard and... thankfully it appeared. I had typed the letter 'h'.

Janet reeled back on her chair. She was in deep shock. I was worried that she might switch the device off or delete the document thinking that she had a virus. She started typing. Over a period of twenty-five minutes this is the result of our first encounter.

Janet:	I don't know how that happened but I am sure this is not happening
Michael:	Y
Janet:	I sense you are present but I am feeling silly and that someone is playing a prank on me
Michael:	N

Janet:	You mean no? You are a very slow typist
Michael:	Y
Janet:	Is that really you. Are you really called Michael Pennington
Michael:	Y
Janet:	Are you dead?
Michael:	Y
Janet:	You want me to leave the wireless switch in the on position?
Michael:	Y
Janet:	Is this how you are able to communicate with me?
Michael:	Y
Janet:	You are obviously having problem with the speed of your typing. I am going to run a virus check on my computer as I am not wholly convinced that this is for real.
Michael:	Y

Janet got up off her chair, ran her fingers through her hair and looked distressed. People were starting to arrive. She had to be careful. I knew that I was on my first step to being able to communicate with the living. Everything had changed. This was nothing short of a miracle.

Janet minimised the word document and went about her work but it was obvious that she found it hard to concentrate. For once, and to add to my frustration, she had a busy day. I could hardly contain my excitement. I wanted to communicate. It would be impossible whilst people were milling around in the office.

Janet had no chance to follow things up. She tried to stay late after work but Peter offered her a lift. He is the accountant. I suddenly went off him. Janet left the word document open and the wireless connection live. It was a Friday and I had all weekend to prepare my next message and improve my skills on the keyboard.

I wrote a message for her to collect on Monday morning:

Janet, I know that you find this hard to believe but please understand that this is really me, Michael Pennington. I need to communicate with you. Something wonderful happened last night and I think it may have something to do with the wireless connection on your laptop. I am not certain but I think it may have a relevance to my ability to communicate in this way.

Typing a message is so slow. I cannot type like you type. I seem to have to concentrate on what letter I want and press what would be to you almost like an imaginary keyboard. I press and concentrate and it works. I am getting better at it. I am mastering how it is working.

I have just visited the BBC web site and read the news on my own. Check your favourites I have bookmarked an article on communicating with ghosts. I really want you to read it. Please try and understand that this is really happening.

Janet I know you sense my being. You are the only one to recognise my existence. Do you realise how important that is for me? I need your help. Do you mind if I create an email account with Yahoo on your computer?

I look forward to seeing you on Monday morning as I always look forward to seeing you, each and every day that you are here. I really enjoy your company and you cannot begin to imagine how much this means to me. I am so grateful that you are helping me in this way.

Yours
Michael

That night and throughout that long weekend I read about electrical energy. I hunted the internet for information. I needed data. I needed lots of it. I had to comprehend and to understand the purpose for my existence and to find out what had happened to me and find a solution. I already had some ideas on what I needed to do next.

The Learning Curve – Michael and Janet

I am really a little anxious about continuing with my memoirs. I hope people are not becoming too concerned with my plight. Please rest assured I am in good spirit and no longer have periods of depression or anger. I no longer feel lonely or desperate. Things have changed. I feel I am being guided.

If something like this had happened to me when I was alive I think it might have driven me to insanity. I have always been a sceptic. The idea of people wandering around trying to make contact with ghosts and the supernatural has always been a subject of fascination and humour for me. Oh how ill informed I had been. If only I had known. If only I had known what I know now.

It was Monday morning and the alarm tone sounded. The usual clinking of door catches and keys. Janet had arrived. She was really early. It was only 7.15 in the morning. I was so glad to see her. I always feel so comfortable in her company. Janet is kind and considerate and always thinks about my welfare. Strange that, I mean what welfare assistance does the state provide for us? Ghosts and spirits have their own problems too you know.

Janet spoke out loud, "Good morning, Michael."

I wish I could have replied.

"Let me just get a coffee and then we can sit down and discuss things before anyone arrives," she said.

Janet arrived at her desk and read my note and she wasted no time in replying. Janet knew that she had no need to type a message in order to reply to me. She only needed to speak.

"Michael, I've thought about this all weekend. I could hardly sleep on Friday night for thinking about what has happened. It all seems like an incredible dream. I know it takes you a long time to reply to me by typing so I'll ask you a few questions and you can reply in text on the laptop. I see that your typing skills have already improved since your last attempt. Have you been practising all weekend?

"I do believe you. The fact that I have seen your typing appear all by itself, and the fact that I can sense your presence and the message that you have left here for me, clearly indicates that you are indeed Michael Pennington. Furthermore, I have found your records at the library. I spent all day Saturday morning hunting and researching information for details about you. You are a hard person to find. I suppose it was a long time ago."

She continued…

"They never did find you did they? I really want to understand you and I hope that you can trust me. If you type out just what you want and guide me, I will only ever take any action based on what you explicitly request of me. Please understand that. I think you do. By the tone of your message I think you know much more about me than I know about you and I would like to get to know you better and to help you. Of course I will open up a Yahoo account for you. Let's do that now."

Janet created a Yahoo account for me. I will not use this to respond to requests to reveal my identity on the internet or enter into direct email correspondence with the living unless I am sure that they are like Janet and can sense my existence.

Janet then leaned back in the chair, moved away from the laptop and waited. I realised she was waiting for me to respond. I seized the opportunity and typed the following:

Janet. Thank you so much.

She must have been bored stiff watching each letter slowly appear on the screen. No doubt though, I was already a lot faster than I had been. I think Janet was conscious of the fact that others would be turning up for work soon, she really had grasped the situation and there appeared to be no doubting her belief in me.

"Michael," she said. She said it in such a way as someone who might be taking charge and control over a situation. Like a commander about to issue a set of important instructions to his troops or a school mistress about to tell a school boy to report to the headmaster.

"You need to write down some details about yourself. You need to tell me everything. Things such as, Why do you think that you are here? Why do you think that I can sense your presence and others cannot? How did you die? What exactly happened to you? What do we do now, and how best do you think I can help you? Are your remains near here? Do you want me to contact anyone on your behalf?"

A sound at the door – the office staff were starting to arrive. Janet shuffled her paperwork around the desk and whispered. "OK, I will leave the word document open. Just write a summary about what has happened to you and minimise the document if anyone comes to my desk in my absence. I will keep an eye on what is going on. Write everything down and don't miss anything out. Let's communicate, Michael. Let's get to know each other."

Peter was in the room. Others were shuffling around too. Janet had considerately drawn up another chair and moved the laptop to the left hand side of her desk. Janet re positioned her paperwork and in-tray, and sat by my side. There she was, creating space for my being. This was in full recognition of my presence. I felt so special. This was space which I didn't need of course. Someone can sit on me, through me, it really doesn't matter. However, it was the recognition that was important.

Janet worked through the day and fussed around, checking every now and then to see what progress I had made. She did this carefully and was able to read snippets between her work and then return, catch up, and go over the information I was giving her. Essentially I was telling her everything I have told you. Right up to my first communication with her. It was a long and laborious process but it had to be done.

I was in my element. I was a recognised person if you could call me a person. I do hate words like spirits and ghosts. I mean I do not have a body or physical presence. Fine. However, it seems unfair to label me with ghost and spirit and classify me as something weird. The thing is, I suppose this is inevitable, as even in the supernatural world we categorise ourselves under these labels too – for want of a better name I suppose.

By the end of the day I had half completed my memoirs on the word document and ended my day's effort with a note to Janet explaining that I did not, at this stage, want any part of this getting any further than for her use only. She confirmed that this was acceptable. Over the next two days I completed my essay and exchanged several long messages with Janet. On the third day she had decided that since I already knew how to communicate through a word document, I would be able to use ICQ, an internet chat applet, to keep in contact with her at home too. Isn't technology a wonderful thing.

Janet spent the next week investigating my case. She traced members of my family who were still living. This was a painful experience for me, and she knew it. She would stay after work and recite details, names and addresses. We would sit there for hours on end with her talking and me replying with an open word document on the laptop in front of us. We discussed my body in the basement. Being alive, her first instinct was to suggest that we got my remains exhumed, but I explained my concerns about this. Janet asked me if I wanted to invite a medium round to the office to try and make contact with me, but I informed her that this was completely unnecessary at this stage as I didn't want some lunatic running around their offices with a Ouija board and chanting. She thought that was really funny and we laughed some. The real reason it was so unnecessary is that, through Janet, I was communicating already.

Janet started to experiment. She had taken on the task with such enthusiasm. She was doing everything she could to help me out. She was hell bent on catching the criminals that had killed me all those years ago. I told her that I thought that this would be an impossible task and that I hadn't even seen them. It had all happened so quickly.

This was before I met Jack of course. Jack is the presence in the building next door, an old engineering shed, recently converted to a repair bay for motorcycles. I hadn't realised that he had died there some fifty years before I had, and that he had witnessed the whole incident all those years ago. If a human had been witness to such events I would guarantee that the details would have been lost or forgotten a long time ago, but Jack, poor Jack, all those years, he was the key to their identity. I was only days away from finding out. We had lived together side by side all those years and he had tried so hard to make contact with me in the past. Anyway, more on Jack later.

Janet continued to stretch the boundaries of both her imagination and mine. We turned off the wireless connection on the laptop and realised that it definitely had something to do with me being able to access and operate the machine. Janet came into the office one day with a handheld palm top computer. She carefully set it up and got me to try to use it. Again, we found that with wireless on, the unit would work. With wireless off it would not function for me. This needs to be investigated as I still have no answers as to why this works. It was at this stage that we discovered that the remote control infra red would access the television and enable me to operate the channels from the palm top. I know you are saying that this is no big deal and that most palm tops do this. No big deal? It was a huge big deal for me. Janet could now leave a television running in the training room and I could sit and watch it. Not only sit and watch it, but I could turn it on and off, and change the channels. That is a big deal I can assure you.

The next milestone in my complete transformation of lifestyle, or perhaps we should invent a completely new word here and refer to it as spiritstyle, was to experience leaving the building. This happened quite by accident and caught me completely unawares. Every day when Janet went to leave I would accompany her downstairs and politely see her off the premises. Janet knew this in the same way that she knew I would wait for her in the mornings, and that I was escorting her as far as I could in the evenings. It was just one way I could express my appreciation for her and let her know that I cared for her.

This particular evening was no different. I followed her down the stairs and waited for her to set the alarm. She opened the exit door. I have no idea why I tried it but I did. The results were not as I might have expected. I stepped outside. Shock horror. I was out. I was gripped by a sense of elation and also of fear. Janet had locked the door. I met with the usual spongy and rubbery feeling that I was used to with barriers or solid objects but I was on the wrong side. I was outside of the building.

Janet was walking away from me at a brisk pace. She had announced her goodbye and she was walking away from the building. What was I to do? Should I follow her? Was that wise? What if I couldn't get back in or I got lost? No, the best thing to do would be to stay there until the following morning and then try and get back inside the building. Any spirit will inform you that time is not really of much relevance under normal circumstances. However, when things become interesting and change with such magnitude, as they have for me, I found that faced with such a situation I was now waiting for time to pass quickly so that I could get back inside to the laptop, and not only that, but I would miss *Coronation Street* as well. It was all so annoying. Why had I been so foolish? What if I couldn't get back in? How had I been able to get out in the first place? So many things were unexplained, and yet, for over thirty years this had been my burning ambition. Nothing made much sense any more.

In some way I realised that a special bond had been formed between Janet and I. With her physical presence I was able to do things that would have been impossible without her being close to me. The ability to pass through a barrier that had previously been impossible could almost certainly and without doubt be attributed to the presence and close proximity of Janet.

I had been spoiled. I was used to my creature comforts and my computer and television. I wanted them back. After a while I became more confident and I decided to explore my new surroundings. I wasn't going to venture far. Just edge round the parameters of the building and see what I can find, I remember thinking. I kept close to the wall and edged round the sides of the building. I reached the canal path. I knew that there was nothing that any living person could do to harm me or cause my death as I am already not of the living. I had no reason to be afraid and yet if I am honest it gave me the creeps and a feeling of insecurity.

I passed quickly by the bricked-up area that had been part of my unfortunate demise and reached the far edge of the building. I looked out over the reflection in the canal water. It was a strange experience. I thought how nice it would be if I could just experience cold or warmth again or feel the touch of water against my skin, even though I knew that was impossible.

The next building had also been smartened up fairly recently. It was the first time I had seen it for so many years. The windows in our office do not allow viewing to the front and back of the building next door. The only view is that of the canal at the rear, the road at the front, and a small section of the area outside the main entrance. It was apparent that people were also working in this building too. They were working late. They were still there. The double doors of the building were wide open and I peered inside and observed two mechanics servicing a smart looking motorcycle. I moved closer for a better look. What happened next is something I shall never forget as long as I have the ability to think and communicate.

As I drew closer to the nearest mechanic, I saw a flash of white light and felt a searing, dragging kind of sensation, which pulled at where my innards would have been if I actually had any. It was like an electrical charge and I actually did feel it. Suddenly it struck me again, and again. It was drawing something from me. I was reeling with astonishment and felt confused and afraid. I was sure it was weakening me. I had to escape. I made it to the open doors but not before I had been struck twice again. I am sure that I heard a kind of gasping and a hissing sound of air as I passed through the doorway. I stared back in disbelief. The workers were still attending to the motorbike as if nothing had happened.

Everything appeared to be normal, and yet it was not. Something or someone was lurking in there. Could it be that one of the men had sensed my presence? This did not explain the strange sensations I had felt. It was then that I noticed a faint aura standing by the open doors. The shape of a person, a small and frail person, yes I was almost sure... there was something else there? Had I finally found someone else like me? If we were alike, then why these strange feelings and no sense of communication? Just a blinding light and a kind of electrical vibrating sensation. It was almost as if my very soul had been touched.

The apparition remained in view all through the night. Long after the doors had been closed and the men had gone home I could see the shape still lingering there. The image was no less weaker for the doors being closed. It would move and shuffle around, returning to the same point at the doors as if in anticipation of my return. I watched it in wonder for most of the night.

At half light I started to edge my way back towards the building entrance. I was not so concerned about getting back in. I had been able to wander around and even enter another building. I had to make sure that I didn't get trapped in such a place though, or indeed anywhere else, for fear of losing contact with Janet. I was careful to not venture too close to the canal edge for I was worried that I might fall in and spend an age wandering along the bottom of the canal for an eternity. This was how paranoid I had become. I wondered how many lost souls were under the water and if things like that actually did happen. I am sure I saw another aura on the far bank of the canal. It seemed to be waving to me. This was unnerving. I wanted the comfort of my home. I had never seen these sights before. I used to look out of the window for years and never noticed such apparitions. Was the presence of a physical barrier such as a windowpane preventing me from viewing such things? No one ever opened the windows at the back of the building. I had no explanation for this or why I could see this figure behind the closed doors. I had no way of knowing that I had just met Jack for the first time.

Janet arrived half an hour early. She was making a habit of this. It gave us the chance to talk and catch up on what was happening before any visitors or staff arrived. I had used ICQ with her twice so far and we would use this chat medium many times in the future.

As Janet arrived at the door she quickly sensed that I was at her side and a sharp intake of breath indicated her surprise. "What are you doing here?" she whispered, sounding confused, as she fumbled to open the door. "I have never sensed you outside the building before, you must tell me what has happened." Janet opened the door and held it open for me. I passed through with ease and Janet closed the door behind us. We both headed straight for the laptop. Little did we know that we were about to open the doors to a whole new universe of active and thriving supernatural activities.

When you know how to contact others in the supernatural world you realise just how much false information is given in the media and in story books. It is all based on supposition. The fact remains that only a spirit can possibly know that he or she is communicating directly with another spirit. A human can understand but cannot possibly know for certain, unless physical proof is provided.

There is one thing that sets us apart that cannot be explained in any book or literature. I wish I could actually convey this to you in more detail, but I find myself completely lost for a way of explaining it to the living. It's a little like trying to explain to someone in a black and white world, the colour green. If you have never experienced colour, and do not know what colour is, then how do you explain to someone what colours are?

The Arrival of Jack and Meeting the Family

When I explained to Janet what had happened she was astounded and became convinced that a presence was haunting the building next door. This is not an unreasonable assumption although I do dislike the word haunting. I also told her about seeing another apparition on the opposite side of the canal bank. Janet decided that she would leave work at the normal time and pay a visit to the company next door. After all, if she could sense my presence, there was every likelihood that she would be able to detect something at another location.

In between breaks and at every available opportunity, Janet and I passed each other messages and planned how we would make contact with the spirit in the next building. How would she explain to the occupants why she was calling round? How would she actually make contact with the presence? Were we leading each other up the garden path? We discussed in great detail how we would make our first approach. Much of this would be based on my own experience of how a spirit might react to its environment. Janet would have to make a good excuse as to why she was calling, and discretely leave a message for whatever was present in the building next door. We finally settled on a suitable message to introduce ourselves to the presence. The message was printed on an A4 piece of paper, in bold type, and read as follows:

Important -- Please Read

My name is Janet. I am trying to make contact with you. Yesterday you were visited by another spirit. I have reason to believe that you are aware of a supernatural visit yesterday. That presence was a Michael Pennington with whom I am in communication with. Michael experienced a violent death in 1971. I am not an experienced medium. I would just appear to be receptive to sensing the afterlife. I do not know how I can establish contact with you without the use of a computer. I do not even know if you are aware of what a computer is. I need to know if there is any way that you can meet up with Michael or find a way of communicating with him or myself. Michael is in the building next door. Can you visit this building? Are you able to leave your building? Michael has found a way of using a computer to communicate with me. I want to find out if I can help you in the same way. I hope that we are able to establish contact.

We didn't know what else to write. The idea was to leave the note in the building next door so that the presence could read it. The difficulty would be in actually getting the occupant to reply and to establish contact. If the presence was trapped in the same way that I had been trapped and without the means or knowledge to access a computer then our plan was flawed. It was all so hit-and-miss.

Janet would have to be very careful how she approached the business owners and what she would say. We agreed that she would be making an enquiry about getting her brother's motorbike serviced. The scene was set. We waited with anticipation for the office to close.

Before I continue with the results of Janet's first encounter with Jack it is only right to comment on certain myths and preconceptions that appear to exist with regard to the supernatural. I am no expert on this subject but I do have the benefit of being in touch with other spirits who are all just as confused as I am as to why certain sightings and photographic evidence just adds to the confusion with regard to the supernatural.

As I see it, if spirits have had the same experience as I have and are desperate to make contact, without the means by which to establish a line of communication, then why would they waste time making silly ghost noises and appearing as apparitions with the sole aim of trying to frighten people. This is assuming that they are even capable of making noises and appearing to humans. I certainly seem incapable of that. I would have made myself known long ago if this was possible. If ghosts and spirits are so lost and confused as to what is happening to them, they would be as desperate as I was to try and establish a sensible channel or medium of contact. The whole idea of ghostly wailings and spooky haunted houses does not appear to make any sense.

I have also contacted many spirits who you would probably class as poltergeists. These are not necessarily evil people at all. Imagine the frustration of years of trying to communicate. If you found a way of moving objects or throwing them around a room to attract attention then surely this does not sound so unreasonable considering the circumstances. It merely helps you to confirm your existence. It is a way of attracting attention. My spirit friend in Leeds would have been classed as a poltergeist. He has explained his amazing ability to actually move and project objects around his environment. This would appear to work in the same way as I am able to project letters onto a document on a computer. It must be based on some form of electrical energy. Another interesting observation is, the older the presence (by this I mean the time since death) the higher the ability to carry out these actions.

Is this to do with each individual spirit's energy levels? The method of death does not appear to have any real significance with respect to each individual's abilities. I have yet to meet any spirit that admits to making wailing noises or confirms that they are able to be seen in human form haunting a building. Janet and I are to experiment with this concept and she is going to attempt to take some photographs of me with a digital camera. I doubt anything will come of it. I cannot see how this will work if she cannot see me without a camera. I should be more positive about these things. Everything is worth investigating.

This leads us to another interesting fact. The number of ghost sightings and paranormal activity would appear to have dropped with the advance of technology and the introduction of computers. My spirit friend Terence from Leeds no longer projects objects around a room and has no wish to frighten the living. Terence is now in communication with others and has no need of this method of attracting attention to himself. Terence once told me of a rather humorous experience he had when he was visited by an exorcist and a vicar from the local church. I cannot say too much or someone will delve into his personal situation. Suffice to say that it did not stop him creating havoc for a number of years. Terence does admit to a mischievous side of his personality by occasionally moving a coffee cup or a book to draw attention to his existence. That is about the extent of his activities today. I can understand this. For my part I am now capable of affecting electrical appliances. More on this later.

If it has taken me over thirty years to find out that a computer is a tool that can by used by the afterlife, and is being used I can assure you, then what of the thousands of other lost souls who have yet to discover this channel of communication. The resources required to track down every spirit or ghost and train the lost souls to open a communication channel is beyond comprehension. There are now many of us that are communicating and I feel that we have merely scratched the surface of what must be one of the most significant breakthroughs in the history of mankind. Who knows where this will lead us and what the future holds. Are we real? We obviously exist, but what are we? Just what is our purpose? I ask myself this question over and over again. Someone has to help us. It is all so frustrating. I digress. On with the details.

The day was drawing to a close. Janet was preparing to leave the office on her mission. I typed one last message on the open word document.

Good Luck Janet.

"Thank you Michael," she said.

I watched as she left. Janet is perfectly capable of filling you in with all the details of how she went about her task but she asked me to convey this to you from my perspective and record exactly what happened when she returned. I do however feel it necessary to explain what happened to her so that you can understand what actually took place and how contact with Jack was established.

By all accounts Janet carried out her mission with military precision. This is how she explained it to me.

Janet recalls the event:

I was nervous. I am not the best communicator in the world. My personality is much more suited to research and study than dealing with people. I am an administrator, a paper shuffler by trade. I prefer the company of close friends and it takes some time for me to formulate relationships with others, so I was not looking forward to having to be devious and lying my way through the forthcoming encounter.

Nevertheless this was an important task and not something that I could ignore. The premises next door are operated by two individuals in their thirties. They are a struggling small business and eke out a living from repairing motorbikes and stocking spares. They are friendly enough and were eager to help with my enquiry over my imaginary brother's motorcycle.

The moment I entered the open doors I sensed a presence. It wasn't something that gradually became apparent. It was strong and powerful from the start. I just knew something was watching my every move. There is no other way of explaining it. Everyone knows the feeling of being watched. This is the best way I can describe it.

I whittled on about costs and enquired about a rough price for a motorbike service. I felt completely stupid when they asked what make and model my brother's motorbike was. This was bad preparation on my part, but easily overcome, by acting in true tradition, like a dumb blonde who was clueless on the subject of motorcycles.

I sensed the presence was extremely close to me. I needed to leave my message in a prominent place or find some way of showing it to the spirit that I sensed was watching my every move. I also had to be careful that I didn't leave it around so that it could be seen by the two mechanics. After all, I had signed it with my name and given information that I was in the building next door. At best, if they found it, they would dismiss me as a lunatic or a weirdo, and at worst, they would come calling and ask to speak to my boss.

I asked them if I could use the toilet. They were slightly embarrassed and one of them commented that it was not the most tidy of environments. Reluctantly I was escorted down a long and dimly-lit corridor to the latrine. You could see that the man was embarrassed about the state of the building, and its grubby walls and floor were what you might expect from a small repair centre. I have been in worse places and it wasn't so bad.

After establishing that the light worked, and fussing around checking that the WC had toilet paper, the mechanic shuffled off back down the corridor to the main work area, leaving me alone standing by the toilet door on a small wooden landing with an exposed and poorly-lit light bulb with which to see. I knew that the presence was close to me. I could feel that it must have been right by my side. I hastily took out the document and held it up in front of me. I prayed that I wouldn't be visited by either of the mechanics and that they would not find me standing there under the light holding up a notice in front of me. Men in white coats sprang to mind as I contemplated the scenario.

I stood there for what seemed like an age. I particularly remember waiting twice as long as it would take for someone to read the notice in an effort to make sure that the message I was trying to convey would be fully understood. I put the notice back in my pocket, entered the toilet, flushed it, and turned off the light.

As I walked back down the corridor I was aware that I was being followed. I bid a hasty farewell to the mechanics who had suspected nothing and I walked out through the open door. I breathed a sigh of relief. It was only when I was half way back to the office that I felt the presence again and a strange feeling of being followed. I looked back but instinctively knew I would not see anything. I desperately needed to get back into the office. I needed to communicate with Michael. Was another spirit following me? Was it friendly? What would happen if it met Michael and got into my place of work. I was nervous and yet excited at the same time.

Janet has documented this encounter in more graphic detail for her own records but I have relayed the content to you so that you can understand how what happened actually took place. From my point of view the results were nothing short of spectacular.

I was waiting by the door for Janet to return. The minute the door opened I realised that her visit had been a success.

That same flash of light and gut-wrenching experience, as an aura of something spiritual, passed by me and made straight down the office corridor. Jack had arrived.

There is much more to tell. How did we get Jack to contact us? I think you already know the answer. How did Jack manage to leave the building so easily? This is due to Janet and is not a common trait in all humans. Janet is a rare individual although there are others just like her. There are also many mediums who are aware of their gift and some very normal individuals who possess the gift and who do not wish to advertise themselves. The good thing about Janet is that she has no wish to offer her services as a medium or to profit from her experience and she is quite content to be of assistance to us and struggles to understand what is happening and how these things work. It is a learning curve for all of us. Nothing is set in concrete. Well, apart from my remains. I trust Janet implicitly.

Whether you are a sceptic or an interested reader, no matter. I hope that you will learn something from my writing. If you do not then I have wasted my time. If sometime in the future you feel that you are not alone then please, do not dismiss this feeling. Experiment. However stupid you may feel it is worth the effort. Keep your findings to yourself until you are sure that what you are experiencing has substance. When you are certain, tread carefully and understand that many would not believe you and that there is no gain in making a fool of yourself. If you do understand, you are a gifted person. You are one of a small minority of genuine individuals with a most wonderful gift and you are of benefit to others. Always act with respect to your contacts wishes. Confirm with them any action you may take and consider the implications from your contact's point of view. This is the best advice I can give you.

I wish you nothing but good will. Enjoy your life and live it to the full. Being alive is a wonderful thing. Breathe deep. Press your hand against your heart. You are alive. This is all that matters. No matter how depressed you may feel sometimes, the worries of finance or personal relationships are things that can be overcome, and, often with regard to material things, are of little relevance. Live for today. You never know what tomorrow may bring.

Many people are interested in establishing the true character of a spirit or ghost. I suppose that you could say, if someone was evil in real life and ended up as a spirit, it is unlikely that they will be any different in character from their original human form. By that I mean they would still be evil. The only difference is that the incentive to be devious and corrupt has been removed by the very nature of our existence. Similarly so, a good person would remain a good spirit. Much of this is indeed in the mind of humans. The human imagination can create demons and bad spirits without any assistance from the supernatural. As an example, a person will take a walk in the countryside on a hot summer's day and admire their surroundings and be thankful that they are enjoying such beauty. Take that same person and place them in the same spot at 2 a.m. at night and they will not be very comfortable. People will often feel afraid and imagine strange and creepy happenings, when in reality nothing has changed. The only difference is that the temperature is cooler and the sun has gone in. Humans should have more fear of fellow beings rather than from the supernatural.

When Jack arrived on the scene that evening it was certainly a most memorable experience. Jack has become a welcome companion to me and a close friend of Janet's too. Jack has mastered the technique of communication and whilst his initial attempts, like mine, were clumsy and incredibly slow, he has learned fast and he is also capable of moving objects. I find this fascinating. Jack has no desire to move back to his old building and is quite settled and at home here with us.

I cannot see Jack, save for the aura that he gives off. To describe it I would say that it is very much like a shadow but with a tinge of the colour yellow. Jack has confirmed that he views me in the same way. Our shapes are not clearly defined but barely visible to each other. It does help us avoid the unpleasant experience of colliding, although occasionally this still happens. Janet continues to feel our presence, more strongly now, but finds it impossible to distinguish between our two spirits or to know which of us is standing by her side. Janet has to rely on typed messages in order to know who is communicating with her. It is a bit like charades sometimes. We have to put our name to text each time we type her a message or she has no idea which one of us is calling her. Using ICQ does help of course. The user name clearly indicates the identity of the caller.

The strange thing is, I have to communicate with Jack in the very same way as I do with Janet. The messages typed on the laptop each day would appear most odd to any onlooker. When you have nothing else to do except learn and chat it is amazing just how much information you absorb and the ingenious way in which you find out about each other. I have an idea what Jack looks like. This is not because I can see Jack, but due to an internet site with pages full of people which I found quite by chance. I scanned through all the images until I found one that looked similar to me. Jack did the same. It was a source of great amusement for us. Jack of course does have the benefit of already having seen me alive.

Jack has no living family left on this earth and spends much of his time searching the internet for other spirits in the hope that he might encounter some old friends or family. This is a long shot, but I can fully understand why he will not give up. Jack is convinced that his own existence is in some way connected with other spirits and possibly my own case and his witnessing of my murder. The accuracy of his deduction would become more apparent to us as my case progressed towards its final conclusion.

Jack's own situation is a strange tale in itself. He was the victim of an unfortunate accident in the building next door. Jack was employed as a machinist at an engineering company and operated a cutting machine up until his untimely death in 1920. For some years prior to his death he had been suffering from poor eyesight, and factory rules and regulations were not as detailed or as safety conscious as they are in modern times. Jack's death was caused by his own negligence, which he freely admits, but he is also at a loss to explain why he is still present as a spirit. There is no crime or accountable reason for why he should still be here. This is probably why he is convinced that my death is connected with his presence here on earth.

There is no possible explanation for his existence that is obvious or logical. Why would Jack be present as a spirit and wait over fifty years to witness my murder? There are many things that cannot easily be explained and are as confusing to spirits as the supernatural world is to the living. What we did not know at the time would become much clearer in the future.

I am already in contact with my own family. For me the task of catching up on thirty odd years is not as difficult as Jack's. My daughter and my wife are fully aware of my existence. They have visited me on many occasions. They are visiting me again this weekend. I have to rely on Janet's hospitality of course, and I know this is taking up so much of her time, but she assures me that she is quite happy with the situation.

The hardest part about meeting up with your loved ones is that whilst you can see them and hear them talk, you are still restricted to having to type messages in order to be understood. Janet had spent the best part of a month tracing my wife who had moved twice and also re-married. My daughter now lives in Wales and she was actually easier to find than my wife. What a shock it was meeting them again. My beautiful wife is now a pensioner and my lovely daughter is entering middle age. I suppose I should have known better. I don't know what I was expecting but it was a strange reunion.

The most difficult aspect of our reunion was having to rely on Janet and her compassion in explaining why she had brought them here to an office in Birmingham to discuss some details about my past. Janet refused to tell them anything in any great detail in advance, and insisted that they actually agree to visit the office in Oldbury and listen to what she had to say. They took some convincing and I am sure that it was curiosity that got the better of them in the end.

Just where do you start to unravel such a strange and surreal tale to the living? How do you break it to them gently that you know the details of what happened to someone who disappeared some thirty years previously? You can imagine their reaction. Janet was good at giving them every minute detail in bite-size chunks. She plied them with strong coffee and delicately spent over two hours going over the whole story. They listened intently, occasionally looking at each other and then back to Janet in disbelief and dismay. At one point I thought my wife, I stand corrected, my ex-wife, was going to leave and dismiss Janet as a disturbed and dangerous person, but it was down to some skilful negotiation by Janet, and the revealing of certain information that I had previously provided her with, that kept their interest from wavering, and assured their willingness to continue listening.

After my family had been provided with all the necessary information, Janet announced that I was in the room with them. My ex-wife was a pensioner now and this was a matter that needed some tactful introduction. As usual Janet was faultless and her caring nature ensured that when the time was ready for me to start typing, they were prepared. That is, as well prepared as anyone can be, considering the circumstances.

I will not bore you with the full details of our conversation or the intimate details I had to reveal in order to convince my wife and daughter that the mysterious type appearing in front of them was indeed their long lost husband and father. There are things that only a family know. There are moments only a family share. This ensured that by the end of the evening they were in absolutely no doubt as to my true identity. From that day forward our relationships have been rekindled and we have had a lot of catching up to do.

Establishing contact with my family has not been easy. I get on much better with my daughter Geraldine who has understood the situation wonderfully and has accepted me for what I am. Thirty years is a long time. Don't imagine that someone can walk away for such a long time and then return and expect everything to be the same again. Of course, in my case this would be impossible anyway.

I do feel fortunate but it also makes me feel sad. I am glad my family know what happened but I do not like to think about the lost years. I did not see my father or mother again and they have passed away. I was not there for them when they were dying. They never had the chance to find out what happened to their son. That is something that I cannot do anything about.

The Witness

One of the first things that Jack was able to tell me concerned the details and account of my own death. Jack had seen it all from the window of the building he was trapped in. Jack remembers every minute detail and he has provided a full description of the culprits. Not much use you would think after all these years. Quite the contrary, it has enabled us, with the help of Janet to build up a very detailed picture of what took place, the names of the people involved, and an exact reconstruction of the murder. The way in which we compiled the details and prepared our evidence required much skill and dedication. There would be a requirement for firm evidence and facts that would need to be painstakingly pieced together and recovered in order to satisfy a jury and convict the culprits of my murder.

Again, I will give you this account in my own words but based on what Jack has revealed to us. Some thirty-three years later, and we are almost at the point where we can hand the details over to the police. This is an eventful period in my existence. Before I continue with Jack's account I will provide you with a little information that may be useful and assist you with your understanding of how things work in the supernatural world.

I do not profess to be an expert with regard to Electronic Voice Phenomenon which is the art of capturing spiritual voices on tape, but I do have details of one particular instance where a voice program was used to solve a particular crime. As far as we have been able to establish it is not possible to record our own voices. We have no voice to record. Converting text into a voice program is possible though, as you will see by the example I shall provide for you.

There is much talk of moving on. Perhaps this is a human urge or an attempt to find security or a reason for everything that happens. Look how my existence has changed. I might actually have more chance of coming into contact with deceased loved ones by trying to find them online. Has anyone considered this? Jack spends much of his time searching the internet and he may end up finding what he is looking for without moving on anywhere. Like me, he has no sense of urgency or ambition to move on. Why should we move on? These are the thoughts that would constantly provide us with much debate and reasoning behind our strange existence.

Many of you will be concerned with investigating my case. Perhaps I am not Michael Pennington. It is possible that there is no Michael Pennington, a spirit from Oldbury. I could have taken any name. I could be Thomas Smith from Wolverhampton. Perhaps this is a prank. I worry that some of you may be a little too concerned about this. To devote any time to discovering my whereabouts and the tracking down of information and records is not the purpose for which my memoirs are written. This is folly. It is irrelevant. It is certainly of no consequence to me and is not in my best interests for you to do so. I have no wish for you to do this or to cause any disruption to our current environment.

Please do not be concerned. There are many good writings that fall under fiction and non fiction that make use of the dead. There are many stories that are concerned with ghosts and spirits and that name them with dates, buildings and information that perhaps should not be revealed. How would the dead react to this if they were alive and could speak for themselves?

If it suits you, treat this as just a story. Put your mind at rest and read it for personal enjoyment or as a means by which to explore more constructive investigation of the supernatural. As I mentioned at the start, I have nothing to gain and nothing to lose by writing this. I do this out of the goodness of my spirit and with all goodwill and the best of intentions. If it excites your mind, questions your theories, encourages you to search and enquire, and most of all, if it pleases you, I will continue. Only on that basis will I devote my efforts to your enquiring minds. If any of you are feeling frightened or intimidated by my writings you should stop. I have no wish to cause alarm.

I fully understand the scepticism with regard to my predicament. Let me first dispel a few myths. A spirit or ghost is not faultless in any accounting or recording of events or documentation, although it is very unlikely that you will find any discrepancies in my records as my memory is excellent. I do not have to clutter my thoughts with worrying about a career, family or the payment of bills and such like. Therefore it is much easier for me to concentrate on issues that are of relevance to my existence.

I can make spelling mistakes and sometimes, though rarely, mix up dates. After all, I think in the same way that you think. I have no idea how I think. I have yet to find anyone, living or dead, who can explain how or why we are even able to function. A spirit can be misguided as in the case of poltergeists. You need to be aware that the supernatural has its limitations too.

Before I continue with Jack's account, I feel I should point out the issue of GCHQ and MI5. How would a mere spirit know of such things? What I am about to reveal has far wider implications and more things for you to consider than my own situation which is insignificant in comparison. It may surprise you to learn that spirits have a much wider access to information than is available to most humans.

Consider how I have found this method of communication. Now think about the number of companies and government departments that have access to much more powerful technology. Of the many people that I am in contact with, perhaps two of the most interesting are spiritual inhabitants of the enormous and sprawling government organisation called GCHQ, based in Cheltenham. Another contact is in the building at MI5 in London. People die in these buildings too you know. A heart attack at work, a construction worker from an existing or previous building on the same site. It happens. We still struggle to understand why we are still around and what forces are at work that prevent us from moving on, if indeed we do move on. It is only in recent times that the answers have become much clearer to us. The importance of computers and the internet to the spirit world are beyond comprehension and the laws of physics as we understand them.

Many of you will find this very far-fetched indeed but it is really no different to my own situation. These spirits however have access to some really useful information that we are able to utilise and pass around to others in our community. It is invaluable when we need to find out about a particular paranormal case or in tracing someone or understanding what the government view is on our strange form of existence.

I will not be providing real names of my contacts as I fear that this is a breach of confidence and, as mentioned earlier, it is up to each individual spirit to decide on what level of publicity they accept. After all, they are perfectly capable of making themselves known to selected persons or human contacts of their own, and indeed do so. Janet is not alone in this respect.

Let us take a look at what is known about GCHQ. If I breach National Security here, and I have no wish to do so, then I apologise, although I hardly think that the information I am providing is a national threat. In any event, sue me. That would be interesting.

In the archives of GCHQ and many other secretive government organisations and the military, there are countless files and dossiers on the paranormal. Many of these relate to UFO sightings but there are also many unexplained, and what you would term, ghostly happenings. If several people were to sight a ghost, or over a period of time a number of people reported seeing the same ghostly phenomena, then it attracts the attention of the authorities. A police officer or member of the armed forces might be asked to log an account and keep quiet about revealing any information to members of the general public. The government will tell you that this is to avoid spreading panic among the population. The truth of the matter is, that all this information is collated and stored. Much of the information sent in from around the country is easily explained. Sightings of UFO and strange noises and transmissions are often near military establishments that are testing new technologies, often at night. Unsuspecting members of the general public are regularly convinced that they have seen a UFO, an alien, or a ghost. This we must accept.

Once this information reaches GCHQ it is categorised and labelled according to its importance. My friendly spirit at GCHQ communicates via the organisation's mainframe computer. This is how we are in contact with him. Our friend was a professor and worked at GCHQ for a number of years before his untimely death. Christopher sees everything and has access to government records. There are no secrets for him. Christopher has to wait until a human reads or writes a report but by looking over someone's shoulder for items that he is interested in he has no problem in gleaning the information. When he is alone he is able to access the data on the organisation's computer. Governments would be paranoid about this if they took it seriously. Be thankful that spirits have no concerns with money or personal gain or the results could have far wider implications for our national security.

The only time I would ever be concerned for the human race being in danger from the supernatural, would be in the event that an evil spirit is present at a nuclear establishment and finds a way of setting off the country's nuclear devices. After all, he or she would have access to everything. To put your minds at rest, this is very unlikely to happen due to the fact that without computers and humans there would be no communication between our kind. Not even an evil spirit would wish to terminate their only means of communication and wander around in a wasteland for eternity. There is also doubt as to whether a spirit could actually instigate the arming, the codes, and the physical side of starting a nuclear strike.

There is an incredible amount of information available that can be accessed. It is in most governments' interest to keep this information secret. The NSA in the United States and other US departments have access to tremendous resources and data on the subject.

There, I have bored you enough. The point I wish to get across is that we do have extraordinary access to information by accessing the world wide web and through our spiritual associates.

There is one more thing that you should know. Ghosts, spirits, a presence, or whatever you wish to call us, and I like the fact that you are kind enough to call me Michael and not ghost or spirit, are much more useful than you may think. How many times have you read in the newspapers about an anonymous caller providing information to the police that has resulted in a conviction or the solution to a crime? It happens a lot doesn't it? Many of these are based on the actions of humans but some are not.

There was a recent incident in Birmingham where a spirit witnessed a violent mugging. No information was available to the police. That is until our friend provided the description and car registration number of the culprit to the police. Jack, Janet and I were absolutely amazed at the ingenious method that he used to report the crime. This particular spirit has no access to any receptive human contact but is able to operate a computer. He is not known to those in the building in which he is trapped. He has no wish to be known to the living.

The secretary at this company uses a voice program where text is turned into voice. The office set-up uses wireless equipment although I do know that this is not essential for communication as other spirits are able to access non wireless systems and microwave as a means of communication. In my case the laptop only works with wireless switched on, although the connection is broadband. A technical issue I am sure. I am not a technician.

Instead of communication by normal text our friend opened up the voice program and typed in the following message before converting it to voice and leaving the open program for her to find in the morning. Imagine her shock and what she must have thought when she listened to her message.

Dear Pauline,

Good morning. I do not wish to alarm you by the fact that you are arriving at your computer to find that it has been tampered with, or rather, used by someone while you have been away but I have some very important information for you.

The fact that someone has been in your office and witnessed a crime should not be a reason for concern as I have no wish to steal or access your premises for any personal motives or monetary gain. Let us just say that I was passing by.

Last night a car parked on the pavement outside your offices and one of the occupants, a white youth, around 5' 6", black medium-length hair and with a goatee beard, wearing jeans, Adidas trainers and a bobble hat, walked about fifty yards down the adjoining side street to the alleyway by the public house that you can see from your manager's office. The man was also wearing a distinctive orange and black anorak and loitered there for approximately five minutes. A bald gentleman, rather portly and carrying a briefcase was walking towards him. As the gentleman drew close, the youth, without warning struck out at the gentleman and produced a knife. It was a sickening scene and totally uncalled for. The victim handed over his briefcase and what looked like a mobile phone and a wallet.

The youth then sprinted back up the road, around the corner, and jumped into the waiting car which sped off immediately. The car was a black Metro. The registration number was… (I omit this in this report for obvious reasons although it was given).

Your first action should be to report this to your manager and then ring the police. After all, your office has also been entered so you must report this crime. If you believe that this is not a truthful account of what happened then you should satisfy your curiosity and telephone the police to enquire as to whether anyone was mugged here last night.

Thank you for your attention.

You can imagine the reaction on the police officer's face when he finally called round to view the evidence. Our friend gives an hilarious account of fingerprint taking of the computer and inspections by the police to find out how the information was provided. Misguided, the manager of the office still thinks to this day that someone hacked into the computer system in order to leave the message. Hardly unreasonable since the building's internal CCTV recorded no intruders.

Suffice to say that the police did apprehend the villains and justice was served. You never really know who is watching do you. Does that worry you? I hope not. We mean you no ill. There are many instances like this. I will inform you later of our very own experience when Jack and I came face to face with a real live burglar. The advantage of being a spirit is the absence of fear of injury. I cannot say the same for the burglar.

I still have not managed to explain to you about the account of Jack in the witnessing of my death and the burglary that led to my discovery that I could manipulate certain electrical items. I am more conscious of time these days. There never seems to be enough time and I have much more time on my hands than any of you.

Let us return to Jack's account of my death. I should not deviate so much from the small part of my memoirs that I am revealing to you.

This is written as Jack explained it to me. It is in my own words and based on his observation of what happened:

For a number of years I would observe my ex-colleagues gradually growing older and working until their eventual retirement. New recruits and trainees would ensure the firm's continuation until its bankruptcy and closure in 1962. The premises remained closed for a number of years before their conversion and renovation in 1997. These were lonely and desperate times and leave me with memories which I would prefer to forget. There is however one incident which shall forever remain clear in my thoughts.

I would watch from every available window of the property in which I was trapped. I spent years with nothing else to do other than watch the world pass by my windows. Time is a valuable commodity when you are alive and a worthless and weary measure of misery when you are alone and without companionship. I would miss nothing and observe every tiny detail. An old man taking a stroll or a couple walking outside would be the sole interest of my attention during those dark times. I have observed the changing fashions and trends of hairstyles and clothes and the wonders of new technology from within the confines of my timeless prison. You cannot begin to imagine the torment and the meaningless state of existence with which I had become accustomed.

I have only ever witnessed one murder. That was Michael's. I have seen pretty much everything else. The violent youths and the playful children using this quiet backwater as a playground for vandalism and entertainment. I even ducked once when they threw a brick through one of my windows. It was the highlight of my day and a great sense of amusement to myself that I had actually tried to avoid the object. I have witnessed the graffiti artists, the boats and barges passing along the waterway, the lovers at night and the day to day happenings of people going about their ordinary lives.

This one day back in 1971 is not something that I shall ever forget. It was a beautiful day and a much welcome break from the previous dreary weather of which we are so accustomed to in this country. Let me first explain the layout of our premises. Please do not take this as a way of finding our location because there have been many changes to the buildings since.

The old boat yard and the building in which I used to reside are side by side and share a joining wall. A towpath or walkway lies to the rear of the building and there used to be a gravel road to the front. The building I was in had an archway and a courtyard which backed on to the canal and the towpath. It was almost hidden and enclosed but with no gate or security to stop entry from the frontage. People working nearby used the premises for parking. The building was vacant for a long period of time until about six years ago when it was renovated. The courtyard could comfortably house around six vehicles which could park with ease within its confines. Part of the building, three floors in height, faces right up to the canal towpath. I used to be able to actually watch people passing right by me and see everything that happened for a considerable distance in either direction.

This one particular day a white Escort van with company markings parked in the car park. There was only one other vehicle present. I had seen the owner on many occasions. I think he worked near here. He is not involved in what happened. The two occupants of the vehicle got out and stood talking by their vehicle. From my vantage point I could not understand what they were saying. They seemed to be arguing about money. I could catch the odd word and I had become very good at lip-reading over the years, but they would not stay still and they were not facing me for most of the time. I saw one of them light up a cigarette.

I have to confess that I did not like the look of them. They were dishevelled and looked like they had been working on a building site. It was obvious that this was their trade due to the rusty and battered nature of the van with its company markings clear for all to see.

The rear of the courtyard had access to the waterfront by a single wooden gate; long gone and rotted away, it has since been completely re-landscaped and improved along with all the other changes that have been made to modernise the building. I emphasise this as I do not wish to encourage people to take a walk along the canal looking for a wooden gate and a building with a courtyard. There was never a lock on the gate and access to the towpath was just a matter of opening the gate.

The two men were acting suspiciously from the start. They had walked over to the gate and were peering through the cracks in the woodwork. After a time, they opened the gate and loitered in the doorway, looking out towards the canal, chatting and smoking.

I decided to get closer and visit my best vantage point by the canal towpath. From there I would be able to see them more clearly as the windows gave an excellent view of the canal and the courtyard. I was convinced that these two were up to no good and my suspicions were to prove warranted. I fully understood of course that if they did do anything untoward there would be nothing that I could do from within the confines of my prison.

I noticed a man walking towards the building along the towpath. Around his late thirties or early forties, he walked briskly and seemingly without a care in the world. I had no idea that I was about to witness a gruesome murder. The two men had noticed his approach and had started mumbling and whispering to each other. They moved back towards the courtyard leaving the gate open. I saw one of them pull out a sharp instrument which looked like a hunting knife.

As the man, which I now know to be Michael, passed the open doorway, the two rogues rushed out and grabbed him from behind. One of them had him by the neck and the other plunged the instrument deep into where his kidneys would have been. It all happened so quickly and I was not prepared for it. I struggled for the best vantage point and saw the man fall to the ground. One of the two attackers kicked and punched the man while he was on the ground and rummaged through his clothing for valuables. I saw them retrieve a wallet and they even took his watch. I watched with horror. These things are horrific, even if you are not alive and in no danger yourself.

I could not believe that something like this would happen in broad daylight. This was such a bold and unprovoked attack. Was this premeditated or something that happened on the spur of the moment? It had certainly looked as if they were planning something from the moment that they had arrived and they were obviously desperate for money. I waited to see what would happen. I heard the following conversation quite clearly as I was now up close and observing their every move from the broken window.

"Shit, Clive, I think you've killed him you idiot," the older man said.

To which the second man, Clive, without a shred of remorse replied, "Quick, George, chuck him in the canal before someone sees us."

"Don't be bloody stupid, he'll drown, and anyway he needs help. What on earth were you thinking of? Why did you use the knife? What have you done?"

George was obviously in shock and distraught at what he had just witnessed. He seemed paralysed with fear and helpless as he watched Clive.

Clive noticed an opening in the building wall next door, a kind of shaft for what must have been a coal bunker used in times gone by.

"Help me quick, drag him over here," said Clive.

George made no attempt to move or to provide any assistance. It was obvious that he had not anticipated his colleague's actions or the situation in which he now found himself in. George was frozen with fear and had a look of remorse and concern for the victim lying on the canal towpath. George watched in disbelief as Clive dragged the body over to the boatyard wall and proceeded to push his unfortunate victim through the open shaft.

I could not see clearly where the hole or entrance to the building was. All I knew was that some poor man was now lying badly injured, dying or dead, in the building next door. As the two men turned to go the man called Clive halted.

"Where's my necklace? Where the hell is my bloody necklace? It's gone. I felt it tugged when we jumped him but that was before we chucked him in there. Quick, find it. It's got my name on it."

The second man stood in a state of paranoid intransigence. His facial expression was withdrawn and ashen as he turned unsteady on his feet and proceeded to be sick against the wall of the boatyard. Clive continued to search the towpath, in an agitated manner.

"It must have fallen in the canal. Forget it, let's get out of here. No one will find him anyway, look someone's on the other side of the bank walking, come on, move it," said Clive.

I could hear them arguing and the second man was full of concern as I heard him suggest that an ambulance be called to try and help their unsuspecting victim. Clive was having none of it and the two murderers left the scene. They did not run, and George was noticeably unsteady in his composure and his gait as they walked back to the courtyard, got into their vehicle, and drove away.

Thankfully, with nothing else to do day after day, the details of the van, its colour, its signage, even the telephone number and number plate, was ingrained upon my memory forever. The memory is an amazing thing when you have nothing else to do but think about the same thing, over and over again. It is not possible to forget such an experience. From that day forward it became a personal mission to retain the knowledge in the hope that some day there would be a way of communicating this information to someone else. Thankfully this day has arrived.

The information that Jack has provided has given us both a sense of achievement. It will not be long before Janet presents the full details of our evidence to the relevant authorities. Contact has already been made. We just wish to find out a little more about what may happen if my body is exhumed. We are in the final stages of our investigations and there is so much more to do and learn before any drastic measures are taken. During this traumatic time we had little knowledge of what was in store for us or what revelations we were about to encounter.

Visitor in the Night

Enough of this, let me tell you about the night we had a burglar. We seldom get such wonderful entertainment and it is rarely in the form of live action such as this. Janet had left us about four hours prior to our unwelcome visitor. We hate it when she leaves. We both looked forward to her arriving in the morning. Janet misses us too you know and even visits us most weekends. After all, she is entrusted with the keys and has access to the building whenever she wishes. The alarm records each individual entry to the premises and each member of staff has a different pass code. Her line manager, Malcolm, assumes that Janet is just using the office to surf the internet as she only has a modem connection at home. There was no indication that this would be different to any other night.

Both Jack and I were sat at the laptop when we heard scuffling sounds and strange noises by the main entrance to the office. We went to investigate. Imagine our surprise when we saw a young man smearing a substance on the window and covering it with brown paper. I think we both guessed what was coming next. Quick as a flash he hit the window with a hammer and in no time he had gained access. The very cheek of it all, we were astonished.

The alarm let out its timer entry thirty second warning. This should be good, I remember thinking. Let's see what he does now. Totally calm, and without doubt an expert, our visitor proceeded to mercilessly smash the alarm unit to pieces. Why was the alarm not sounding outside? As he snipped the cables of the main control unit we could hear a muffled alarm going off outside but it was not very loud at all. We found out later that the alarm siren had been packed full of quick drying foam sealant of the kind that they use in cavity walls and for filling big gaps. This was certainly an effective method of disabling the alarm system.

It suddenly dawned on me that we had to do something and I was thrown into a complete sense of panic when I realised that the laptop was about to end up in this character's swag bag. I ran down the corridor back towards where we had been sat. Just quite what I was going to do I had no idea. Type a warning at him? Hmmm, not quite an effective means of deterrent. Even though I am not of the living I was quite surprised at my level of energy. It was almost like an adrenalin rush only more of an electrical charge. Was this because I had bounced off Jack about four times in my haste to return to the laptop or because the situation somehow gave me a heightened sense of awareness? More importantly, just what would we do now? I need not have worried.

The intruder grinned as he saw the laptop but he made straight for the manager's office. I knew he wouldn't leave the laptop but it bought me some time. As a human the very thought of turning to the keyboard to start typing in the middle of an emergency must be quite amusing. For me it was an act of desperation and I wanted to ask Jack what course of action we should take and did he have any ideas? I typed in earnest.

Michael:	Quick what the hell are we going to do?
Jack:	This could be interesting
Michael:	What do you mean interesting? Do something!
Jack:	You worry too much
Michael:	I DON'T WANT TO LOSE THIS LAP...

I never quite finished. Our intruder was back in the main office having obviously rifled what he wanted from the drawers in the next room. The youth had already filled half a large sack full of stolen goods and was making straight for Janet's desk. A feeling of despair came over me as I became convinced that we were about to lose the laptop. This is where things became fun.

I watched the young man approaching the desk and suddenly come to an abrupt halt about three feet from the where I was stood. His nonchalant and relaxed manner was suddenly transformed and his face became a picture of abject horror. His eyes boggled and his jaw dropped. I looked at the desk. The sight of a stapler suspended in mid air imitating the motions of a snake head and hovering from side to side and facing him head on must have been terrifying. Good old Jack, my hero. The guy was amazing. I was full of envy and pride at the same time.

The youth bolted down the corridor. A heavy paperweight rose gracefully from the table, arched around in a curve, and shot off with the speed of a bullet. It swiftly negotiated the fleeing burglar and smashed with a terrific force against the wall by the entrance door. The youth was petrified. He was literally wetting himself and froze in fear. The paperweight, in two halves now, rose from the floor and hovered by the only exit from the building. The young man turned and fled back into the main office and into the darkened room of the company accountant. How I wished Janet could have left all the lights on, I would have been able to see things more clearly I thought. This was exciting. The lights mysteriously came on, seemingly of their own accord. Marvellous, Jack was a genius.

The youth was struggling to break the lock on the handle of the window and make his exit. Pretty risky to jump from this height I thought, but at the same time I could see the desperate look of fear on the burglar's face. Jack had obviously had difficulty balancing each half of the paperweight and he was back on the attack with the stapler now. Into the room it went and hung menacingly about three feet from its victim. I actually felt sorry for the poor unfortunate person that had been subjected to this assault. However, my compassion was short lived. After all, he had not been invited. He was an unwelcome guest. The young man had slumped to the ground and curled himself up in a defensive ball against the wall, presumably for comfort and protection. Even when Jack let the stapler settle on the floor he made no attempt to move or escape. He remained as good as gold and sat in the room until morning.

When Janet arrived she was shocked to find that the offices had been broken into. She was even more surprised to find our victim sat quietly in the accountant's office. Janet was not the first to speak. The youth pleaded with her to call the police and keep the stapler away from him. When we later explained all this to Janet she told us how proud she was, and how meeting us had changed her life. That was such a nice thing to say.

While Janet phoned the police, Jack steered the two halves of the paperweight back to their original position. The youth closed his eyes tightly and refused to watch this amazing feat. We knew someone would notice that the paperweight was broken but we also knew that it was no big deal to find a broken paperweight in an office. The most worrying aspect was how seriously the burglar would be believed with his description of what had happened. During all this time the youth sat waiting and never attempted to make an escape. He was anxious that the police arrive before he would move. He was taking no chances. I could see Janet was enjoying the moment. Within easy listening distance of the burglar she said, "Thank you boys and behave yourself now, stapler, the police are on their way." I made my way to the laptop. Jack was already there. He had already left me a message.

Jack: Michael we should have more nights like this. That was fun.

Michael: Jack you are a hero. I feel so useless against your awesome skills. What a performance. The speed of the paperweight was fantastic. Did you see his face? Brilliant work. I never thought a stapler could be so

	menacing and you must have been reading my mind the way you operated the lights.
Jack:	Thanks Michael but we were a team. I don't do lights. No idea how you managed that. It wasn't me. Well done, my friend.

What? Doesn't do lights? Surely not. I walked over to the room where the youth was. I switched off the light. It was as simple as that. It just switched off. Our visitor twitched, jumped nervously, and called once again for Janet to call the police because they were taking too long. I felt good. It had been an eventful night.

The police arrived and the burglar looked so relieved. The police were baffled which was hardly surprising. Comments were made that the youth looked as if he had seen a ghost. The young man adamantly refused to tell the police what had happened. He wanted the police to take him out of the building straight away. He kept nervously glancing at the innocent stapler which was now in its rightful place on Janet's desk.

We seldom have nights like this. Oh what fun it was.

I can obtain all kinds of information. Almost anything in fact, so long as I have a spirit contact in the right location. If I do not, there is always another presence that will know of a spirit that can assist. This is a well organised network that spans the globe. I am often heavily criticised by my peers for my actions, which has in the past been a source of discomfort to me. Historically it has not been in the spirit nature to draw attention to oneself and I have certainly exceeded myself by offering my memoirs for public consumption. I have however, also proved them wrong on many occasions and there are others that are now supporting me in this cause. It is fortunate that the majority of you are sceptical and that it is assumed that I will not be believed or this global and organised program might have been shut down long ago. As mentioned previously, this could all be a hoax.

Perhaps the most useful contribution that the spirit world can provide to the human race is one of historic interest. Just because a spirit inhabits a lab does not mean that he or she can carry out effective research. I would of course refrain from trying to pick up a test tube. Jack would probably fare better at this I feel. Many spirits marvel at the advances of technology and are in awe of the clever minds behind new discoveries. Little did we know that we would soon be subjected to information that was beyond our comprehension.

Whilst millions of pounds of your taxes are spent in armaments to provide cannon fodder for the afterlife, there are organisations that could help bond the ties between the spirit world and the living and which are laid waste and discarded as insignificant entities of no merit. In time this will change. For the present this is something we have to work around.

The Mission

As a result of this experiment in communication over the internet, I have now established contact with three more lost spirits and two very helpful humans with abilities beyond the accepted norm.

There are rules and established methods and lines of communication between the spirit world and the living. We have not broken any rules. We have just edged a little closer towards the outer circle of what is deemed to be an acceptable barrier between our two worlds.

Alas, I have not yet found a genuine and experienced medium on the internet. Perhaps I should have provided more signals so that they would have understood. No matter. This kind of matching between human and spirit is happening all over the country. You should be aware of it. Not only in this country, but all around the globe. This is an organised and orchestrated mission that will change the course of history. Of that you should have no doubt.

The interest that my case has created in both the spiritual world and the world of the living is intriguing. I would have expected this more in the land of the living than I would have done in the spirit world. However, it would seem that we are as inquisitive alive as we are dead. I have had approaches from some of my contacts about their own experiences. Both Jack and I are in constant contact with other spirits with similar tales and experiences to tell. The word is spreading slowly to all corners and countries of our planet.

Calling the Spirits

Incidentally, and whilst on this subject, I can confirm that I am very suspicious of many commercial mediums and charlatans who claim to understand the supernatural. There are many instances on record where a spirit has witnessed the most amateur of ghost hunting practices. These involve lights, video recorders, tape recorders and a host of seismic equipment that would put the film *Ghostbusters* to shame. I have watched this most humorous film.

I can recall the topic of conversation with a spirit friend of mine who experienced a group of ghost hunters, going to great lengths to fabricate digital images on a camera, so that they would have some evidence to show their club members the next day. These were ordinary people who had probably set out to obtain the truth and been misled and misguided by more strong-willed thrill seekers seeking recognition for their efforts.

There is much made of Ouija boards and the dangers of calling up the spirits via this medium. Look at this from a different perspective. Let me provide you with an example that Jack proposed. Consider that you had been trapped in a house or building for a long period of time. That building may have been empty or inhabited but you had found no way of communicating with the people that resided there or you had been alone for years waiting for some excitement.

Without warning and out of the blue you see people huddle around a table and prepare for a calling of the spirits. A professional psychic medium is going through his pre amble and setting the scene for the calling of the dead. I have no objection to humans trying to make contact, we actively encourage it, but this particular fellow hasn't even acknowledged or felt that a spirit is actually watching him from within the very same room. Obviously a fake medium. This is an outrage. An insult to our existence. Instead, he dishonestly claims to feel that he is being contacted by some long lost soul who died in the house and yet isn't actually present at all. He starts to ramble about how she is happy and proceeds to say nice things about her to his audience. In Jack's own words – things would start to fly. Should an unlucky medium meet a spirit with Jack's abilities I would be very worried if I were he or she. And you wonder why Ouija boards are dangerous? Do not dabble in things that you do not understand.

Many of you will be thinking about your own abilities. The fact of the matter is that you will probably have an inkling already. There are a few examples of how you or others can tell if you are suited. You cannot use these examples as absolute proof and you should not convince yourself that you have 'the gift' just because all or one of them apply to you. If all of them apply to you then I would suggest that you experiment further. If only one or two of them apply then it is likely you may be using a part of your being that others cannot. The examples given here are not exhaustive and I refrain from passing on more detailed indications of a person's ability that would class them as 'gifted' by the afterlife:

Consistently, for both close friends and relatives, but more importantly with regard to strangers – knowing what someone is about to say before they say it.

You are sitting in a chair watching the television and you know that someone is about to knock on the door or ring the bell before they do.

You think about the phone ringing and then suddenly it rings. This should be a regular occurrence.

Whenever someone is watching you your senses have a habit of telling you. Be wary of this one because this is a common ability.

You regularly experience the feeling that places that you have never visited are familiar and that you have been there before. This is very important and there is a reason behind this that I will not divulge at present.

How would anyone know who is alive or dead online? This is exactly how we can hide. I can enter a normal chat room unannounced and partake in the conversations of the living with the same ease as I enter the chat rooms frequented by the dead. If I wish to discuss something with a known spirit then I enter private chat. You have no idea how technology and the internet has mobilised the spirits in a way that would have been impossible only a few years back. Only now are humans coming to understand that it is not always in their best interests to conform with what we are conditioned to believe through our education system and peer pressure. Be an individual. Work things out for yourself.

Previously I mentioned that my memoirs have caused great interest in the spirit world. I have no shortage of content and offers from spirits wanting to provide their assistance. Why don't they all just write their own stories and get on with it you ask. Well, in some cases they do and are doing just that. Others require better literary skills to put down what they have to say in the right format. In most cases when in contact with humans they are not taken seriously so they regard their efforts as futile.

There are many questions I do not answer this time. I will complete my memoirs and then perhaps you will understand the full story in a way not possible in this fragmented environment of extracts from a message forum online. I have given you many things to think about.

There are some things which remain unclear and which I fear is a cause for confusion for some readers. I am not a medium and cannot claim to have powers of communication with other spirits by thought process. If you are desperate to make contact and you are trying too hard then I fear that contact may not transpire. If you are a genuine medium then you will know that it is only correct to discuss your findings in private with the individuals concerned. If I were to pass a message on to someone at the request of a spirit I would do this with the utmost care and confidentiality.

I do have some ability, whether psychic or otherwise. This is perhaps not the correct term and should remain in the domain of humans but our electrical energy is beyond the comprehension of many. The very idea that a spirit is communicating with you via the internet or a chat program is more than a little unbelievable.

With regard to your possible interest in contacting others, there are many of you that I feel have an ability in this field, and I understand that you are keen and willing to explore the process of making contact with others from the afterlife. I can only relay to you my own experience of how this works, the nature of which is contained within my past and current writings. If you are in the presence of spirits or the unknown and you strongly sense their being, then I would urge you to act with a degree of constraint. Your contacts are most probably very pleased to have your company and take an active interest in your person and your well being. If you are experiencing these feelings then you are indeed a special person. I have merely passed on to you my own method of communication and how it works for me. There may be some very valid reasons why you are unable to make contact with others.

Let us take a look at what may be happening and the underlying reasons why contact is not as simple as it may seem. As an example, once contact had been established with Janet, it still took me some time to discover that I could communicate with her through a computer. I had already been observing people using computers for some weeks prior to this chance and amazing discovery. Despite this, I still have to communicate via a particular laptop with a wireless connection. I cannot operate a standard PC and keyboard. Please do not all rush out and purchase such items as this would be an expensive exercise. I do know that there are others like me who communicate on normal PC equipment.

If you have left a clear messages to a presence or spirits that you believe are with you, and following the same procedure as Janet you have made attempts to contact your 'friends', then do not be disheartened if the results are not forthcoming. It may be that those present cannot operate your equipment or cannot sense that you feel they are present. If they do feel that you sense their being then this may be enough for them and they may have no wish to contact the living.

For my part I continue to endeavour to establish contact with the lost souls that are around us. I am making considerable progress in this field. One day you will happen upon an article on the internet or a forum somewhere and recognise my style of approach. The story may be similar to my own but in different circumstances or on a different continent, but the aim will be the same. You will smile and understand. I hope you will have fond memories of me. Regardless of what happens to me. this message will be passed on to others and my efforts will not be in vain. As previously mentioned, many have now joined me and the message is spreading.

Some day in the not too distant future and during most of your lifetimes the whole subject of spirits and ghosts and the paranormal will be explained. The human race has made great progress in this arena and it will not be long before our network announces its existence to the living. There will be a most eventful and historic day that will come to pass and history will be rewritten. Governments and nations will unite in a way that would be impossible in today's climate. You will have been part of that. You will think back and remember Michael. It will all make sense to you. My mission will have been worthwhile. For the time being let us consider that this account of my life and death are the ramblings of a fool. No matter. I do not take offence at this suggestion. It is of no relevance.

One thing that you may find strange and that death has taught me – if I were to live my time again as a human being, would I change anything? I most certainly would. The stupidity of my selfish existence as a human is easily observed with hindsight. Such a pity that I was not privy to what I know now. Worldly possessions and the quest for material goods are a poor substitute for love. Embrace your loved ones. Money cannot buy you happiness. It may seem to help misery more easy to cope with but that is a false delusion. Some of the happiest people in the world are poor.

To the evil of this world I serve warning. The mad mullahs of the Islam world hiding behind a wall of deceit and self-opinionated prophecies and the fanatics of the Catholic and Protestant religions with their fire and brimstone speeches. Religion, in history, has caused more strife and premature death than any World War. I make a sweeping statement in that I can confidently say that I am more religious than many of you who use religion for political gain and advantage even though I embrace no particular Church or religious creed. If you abuse your religion there is little hope, empathy or understanding waiting for you in the afterlife. Islam, Christianity, Jewish, Sikh or Buddhist. Which is the chosen religion? Does it matter? Embrace them all if it pleases you but do not use them for devious and incorrect interpretations of their meaning and the love that they can inspire.

The Investigation Commences

I am beginning to sound like a prophet of doom. This was not my intention. Perhaps brought on about concerns I have for my own future. I do not know what the future holds for me. I still seek to find old and ancient spirits who have experiences of times long gone in the hope that they might provide me with more substantial evidence of the meaning of life and death.

At this point I feel it is wise to continue with the details of my own situation.

With Jack having provided us with the details of my eventful passing, we were now in a dilemma as to what course of action to take. We know that one of the perpetrators of my demise from my human form has conveniently left us with a locket and a name. The fact that this lay somewhere in the shifting silt of the canal waters was a matter of some concern but if it were a gold locket or a silver locket there was every possibility that the murderers could be brought to justice.

While you were all enjoying your Christmas break our beloved Janet was spending her time back and forth from libraries and registrar offices compiling information that would be needed to trace our targets. Janet compiled a detailed and accurate document for the police and managed to find the current address of one of the two men that had killed me all those years ago. The other has since died. I had more than a few words I would like to have conveyed to this individual if I ever come across him in my journey around the spiritual world. I am not a vindictive personality by nature and I would not wish to torment his soul but I did have spirit friends on the look out for him. I did not realise that my wish would come true but in an entirely different manner than I could have foreseen or expected at the time.

We discovered that one of the murderers, by the name of Clive Mellows, was living in Newtown in Birmingham. With amazement and a feeling of awe and intrigue, we gradually collated the information and went about our investigations. Janet, much to our concern at the time, even paid the street a visit and observed the individual concerned walking to the post office. Armed with a digital camera, and sitting in her car with the window open, she took several photographs of him for our perusal. Jack was able to confirm that whilst the years had taken their toll, this was indeed one of the men that had been responsible for my death.

The scene was set but we were now in a quandary. How would we actually approach the police? How would Janet explain how she had come about the evidence? This would obviously draw attention to the company and would not go without notice. There was no concern that Janet would be arrested in connection with my disappearance as she was but a mere child at the time of my passing. However, the nature and the circumstance by which this evidence had come to light would be the most difficult of problems to overcome. It would not be possible to just ring up the police and call them round. You cannot expect the police to act upon such scant evidence and supposition, let alone expect them to embark upon digging into a building's foundations and dredging a canal. This was obviously something that required much skill and delicate handling.

The truth had to be revealed but it was no simple matter. Jack was now becoming very concerned with the turn of events. At best he might lose his closest spirit friend and at worst he might be faced with exorcists and misguided attempts to assist him in moving on. We had major concerns which we discussed and debated considerably in advance of our provision of this information to the police.

And what of me? I had my own concerns. Just what is heaven and hell? What actually happens to us if we move on? There is no guidebook and nothing conclusive that has been written or proven with regard to this. It is all based on supposition. It was a very harrowing time and I am sure Janet did not have a very enjoyable Christmas as a result. Dear Janet, she always puts on such a brave face with regard to these matters.

Whilst Jack and I struggled to come to terms with the possibilities and likely outcome of our quest, Janet reasoned that we would need additional assistance and some tactful negotiation from another trusted human who had no ability or gift with respect to the supernatural.

Janet's boss, and the business owner, is a pleasant and jovial individual of middle age. David is a practical man and a no-nonsense businessman. He has been successful though he does not flaunt his success. We know he has a great respect for Janet and he is always careful to treat his employees with kindness, whilst maintaining a firm grip on the day-to-day running of his enterprising and profitable organisation. Most importantly, he is approachable and is a great listener. This would make our task a little easier. It all depended on David now. Janet would approach him with a view to discussing our predicament. This was also the most honourable thing that we could do considering we were his guests, residing at his premises, and about to cause a major disruption to his business.

After the Christmas break and after much debate and conversation between Jack and I, the office staff returned to work. Janet had of course spent most of Christmas and the New Year with us, rushing off for Christmas dinner and time with her family in between long days at the office and investigating.

Janet wasted no time in approaching David. She explained that she had a very delicate matter that required his confidential attention and that it was something that would require his full understanding and cooperation. She is not normally an assertive person and both Jack and I admired the way she captured his attention. It was agreed that David would discuss this with her after work when the other staff had gone home.

Jack spent most of the day hovering around David to see if he would discuss this with anyone or breach Janet's confidence by asking questions of others. Malcolm, Janet's line manager, had noticed Janet close the door to speak to David and was inquisitive as to the nature of Janet's enquiry. David's only acknowledgement was that it was a personal matter that he would be discussing with Janet after work. "I hope she isn't going to leave us" was his only comment to Malcolm.

A day can pass slowly for a spirit too. With so many things to observe and view during a day at a busy office, this was not normally a problem, but this particular day dragged on and on and made me impatient. The time came and Janet was summoned to David's office. With a great deal of curiosity and a sense of unease, Jack and I stood side by side with Janet so that our presence and our support could be felt by her. This was no easy task for Janet. Everything relied on Janet and David's reaction now.

What you are about to hear are the exact words from the conversation that took place between Janet and David.

"Come in Janet, grab a seat, no need to stand on ceremony," David said.

"Thank you David, I know this is a little unusual but I have something to tell you and I don't know where to begin," Janet replied.

David spoke with an enquiring tone. "At the beginning would be good then. Just fire away and let me know what is on your mind. I have an idea what you are about to tell me anyway but I hope I'm wrong."

"David, I don't think so, I don't think you could possibly know what I am about to tell you and what worries me is what you will think of me afterwards," Janet replied with a degree of anxiety in her voice.

David looked worried.

"I hope it's not a personal problem or a woman thing Janet. I'm not good at that type of conversation, are you sure that I am the right person you should be speaking to?"

At this point Janet could take it no longer and burst into tears. This took both Jack and I by surprise and David shuffled nervously in his chair as he struggled to work out what to do next. Janet regained her composure and continued.

"In some ways what I am about to tell you is very personal. I have two friends whose very existence may depend on what you decide to do as a result of what I have to say. I don't know how to begin because if someone were to tell me what I am about to tell you then I would be very worried about them. The only reason I am telling you is that I have to. I have no option. I can also prove that what I am saying is based on fact, although this in itself will give you reasons for being very concerned.

"I have never lied to you and I like to think that I have done a good job whilst I have been working for you and I would hate to lose your friendship and have you dismiss me as a lunatic or someone who should seek therapy. If you can just bring yourself to consider that what I am about to tell you is justified and take the necessary action then I will be indebted to you for the rest of my life. This is how serious I am about the subject and yet I still do not know where to begin."

David had listened intently to Janet's words and he looked nervous, but at the same time we could tell that he was receptive. Would his attitude change as the story unfolded?

David spoke firmly and deliberately and was being as tactful as he could. "Janet, I have known you for some time now and I want you to know that I am honoured that you have chosen to tell me whatever it is you are about to explain. I like to think of myself as an open-minded and approachable person so whatever it is you want to say just spit it out, girl, and let's discuss it."

"What worries me, David, is just how open-minded are you and how good are you at keeping a secret and taking action on my findings," Janet said.

David replied. "Let's get one thing straight, Janet, the fact that you have approached me in this way and are obviously very worried about something leads me to assure you that nothing you tell me will go outside these four walls unless you want it to."

Jack and I listened and waited for Janet's skilful and tactful explanation and did not expect her to come out with the truth in quite the way that she did. It was so direct and straight to the point. This was so unlike Janet, who was now finding the conversation stressful.

"David, this place is the scene of a murder that took place in 1971. The body is in the basement or cellar area of the building that has been bricked up. There is a necklace and a locket with the murderer's name on it in the canal. I have two spirits or ghosts that I am in contact with who are with me right now and I have the name of the person who committed the murder all those years ago and I desperately need you to believe me and help me."

David sat in disbelief and stunned silence. Not a word was spoken for what seemed like an age. This was not going to plan. Janet was sobbing uncontrollably and not handling the situation as well as we might have expected. It had all been too much for her. David coughed nervously and was the first to speak.

David replied in a rather shaky and unsteady voice. "Janet, I really don't know what to say. I never expected you to come out with something like this. Let's calm down. I need to think about this."

David swivelled round on his office chair and opened the lower drawer of the filing cabinet. He produced a bottle of brandy and two glasses. Slowly he poured both himself and Janet a double brandy and placed the glasses on the desk. He was trembling and obviously shaken by what he had just heard.

Janet was still sobbing and finding it difficult to speak. "I knew you wouldn't believe me. I knew it. I'm so sorry."

"Janet, have you any proof of this?" David said.

"Yes, it can be proved but I don't know if you are ready for it," Janet replied.

David now spoke with a kind and soothing manner, he was still unconvinced. "Well, apart from the fact that this has to be the most extraordinary thing anyone has ever told me in my entire life I am all ears," he said.

Janet stood up. Jack and I nervously careered into each other and I felt the electricity of our contact. Janet dashed out of the office leaving David sat in amazement until she returned clutching the laptop. Instantly Jack and I knew what she was doing. If nothing else this could save the day. Janet placed the laptop on David's desk. She opened up a word document and typed a simple statement.

> Boys it is up to you now – help me

To which I typed:

> David, this is Michael.
> I am pleased to communicate with you.

If ever a man could have died of fright then this was the time. Instead, David stared horrified at the screen with disbelief, grabbed his glass, and in one huge gulp he swallowed the contents and topped it up again. Not a word was spoken between Janet and David for several minutes.

David took charge of the laptop. He turned if off and then back on again. He checked for any new or unusual programs in the start menu and opened up a new word document. He typed the following message.

> If this is a joke then it is the best prank I have ever seen

To which I replied:

> Well no one could have known what your manager was asking
> you about Janet this morning unless they were in your room.
> You thought she was going to leave didn't you. What proof do
> you need? How can I convince you?

David sank back in his chair. He looked tired and withdrawn. He turned to Janet and spoke slowly and with deliberation.

"Janet, I have to get my head round this. This is messing with my mind. Start from the very beginning and tell me everything you know. Let me just ring home and tell them I am going to be late. You have my undivided attention."

That was how it was. I mean how else could we have explained it. Janet filled in the intricate details of how we had first met, how Jack had arrived, who we were and what we thought. Throughout all of this David sat intently like a child hearing a fairy tale. And who could blame him. After all, this was the most incredible and mind-blowing experience of his entire life. Think how you would feel.

David has become our close friend. In some ways he is a changed man. His attention to detail and his love of life has become a passion. David is still running the company effectively but his aspiration for wealth and riches has dwindled. David still takes his responsibility seriously and understands that he is providing much needed work for his employees.

Both David and Janet now plotted and planned their approach to the authorities. David knows a senior police officer at West Midlands Police. It would be far better to use his friend to explain the circumstances behind this strange tale than make a more conventional approach and have PC Plod running amok around his office asking embarrassing questions and ripping the building apart. We had every faith in David. It was not going to be an easy task as you will see. We had however, made the right decision.

David made the necessary arrangements for his friend from the police force to call round on the following Saturday morning. David contacted his brother who owns a small building contractor firm and hired a dredger barge for the following weekend. The wheels were in motion. I am approaching the conclusion of the discovery of my remains and the trauma and frustrations of the enquiry that followed.

The serving of a D notice and my subsequent recording on a dossier by the Government has led to certain parts of my account being classified under the Official Secrets Act. I do not believe that what I have to say is of national concern nor indeed any threat to the security of this or any other nation. However, the powers that be have made certain assumptions and do not regard my case as something that is best discussed with the general public. Apparently it is not in the public interest to reveal my accounts or to allow for general distribution.

It is not possible for this or any government to hide what I or other spirits have to say. However, it does not suit my cause to spread panic or any form of disruption at all.

The final chapters of my memoirs cover the investigations that took place recently over that weekend and the subsequent enquiry that ensued. As you will be aware, David had made certain preparations. That weekend was a most eventful experience for all of us.

During the course of the week both Janet and David had discussed how they would explain things to the Police Inspector. Whilst David had been shown proof of my existence, a much greater degree of care and attention would be necessary when dealing with the authorities.

The eventful day arrived. Jack and I were extremely nervous about the whole situation. This was uncharted territory and we were venturing into the unknown. At around 9 a.m. in the morning we observed a small tug, about half the size of a narrow boat, with a metal tripod-like frame, a dredging bucket and bristling with chains and cables. This was not a full-sized dredger as we might have expected but it would only be required to trawl a small area of the canal.

David spent some time briefing the crew about what they were going to be looking for. They were surprised that so much trouble was being taken to find such a small object and expressed their concern that it might be a little like trying to find a needle in a haystack after so many years. In any event, they would have to wait for the police to issue them with instructions to commence their search.

The next to arrive were the builders. David wasted no time in authorising their entry to the sealed-off area that would lead to the basement or cellar, and they started work on removing the bricked-up doorway that had once been the entrance to my tomb. The builders were asked not to disturb the ground or make any attempt to dig into the concrete or rubble that they might find on the floor or within the cellar area. Both the crew of the dredger and the builders were not privy to the reasons as to why they had been called.

Finally, at 9.45 a.m. the Police Inspector arrived. This was what we had been waiting for. David was nervous and embarrassed. I had never seen Janet so worried before. I will not trouble you with the intricate details of the conversation or the laborious preamble that David used before he could finally bring himself to explain what he had witnessed and show the inspector the report that Janet had prepared.

When David had finished explaining everything the inspector just smiled.

"David, I have known you for how many years now? In all that time I have regarded you as one of the most straight forward and honest people that I know. But you cannot possibly expect me to believe all this nonsense."

David replied, "No I can't. But you could as a friend be kind enough to at least humour me and wait until we establish what may or may not be down in the basement can you not?"

The inspector calmly replied, "Fine, David, you seem to have gone to a lot of trouble to organise this but look at it from my point of view. You have no hard evidence to back up the story and you have no proof, as yet. I seriously doubt if there is anything at all in the basement and I think you have been the victim of a very elaborate hoax. Someone is definitely pulling your leg on this one."

David was determined to continue, "Please, just humour me on this one. Can I ask the crew of the dredger to start their search and for the builders to look for the body or what remains of it?

"It may take some time but we do know which area to look. I have ordered lunch from a local sandwich bar. We could be here for a while."

The inspector was obviously amused. "OK, David, I don't make a habit of passing my weekends in this way but to give you peace of mind and settle this once and for all, I can put up with it. I think you are being more than a little irrational and smashing down a wall like this, damaging your offices and hiring a barge is taking things a bit too far if you want my opinion. Let's take look at the basement first. I don't think we really want to start dredging a canal without having found something in the cellar do you? In the unlikely event that anything is discovered we have our own people who can do this work."

David instructed the builders to commence excavation of the corner of the room opposite to where the outside entrance had been bricked up. The builders were well prepared having brought all the necessary tools and lighting to make their task easier. I could not bring myself to venture down into the room. Even after all this time I was fearful of what might happen and more than a little repulsed at the thought of having to view what may be left of my remains. Jack was not so nervous about this and observed the excavation work.

It was apparent that whilst a lot of rubble and concrete had been poured into the basement, the pneumatic drills were making short work of removing large chunks of concrete and debris from the area where I had been incarcerated.

The concrete used was not of good quality and by lunchtime the builders had made considerable progress.

The inspector had become bored and found it necessary to disappear on a couple of occasions to purchase newspapers and visit the local shops.

When lunch arrived, talk turned to football and every day more mundane matters and niceties. It was obvious the inspector was amused with the whole concept and the extraordinary efforts being made to dig into the foundations of the building.

One of the builders appeared. Ashen-faced, he turned to the inspector.

"I think you had better come and have a look at this, sir," he said in a shaky voice.

"Have you found something?" the inspector replied in an astonished and enquiring tone.

"I think my job's done here. No one said anything about digging up bones. I'm a builder not a fu****g grave digger. Sorry but I don't like this at all," the builder nervously replied.

The inspector was clearly shocked and he looked at David and Janet in turn before venturing down into the basement. When he returned he had a sense of commitment and purpose.

The inspector turned to David.

"David, I think the situation has quite clearly changed considerably with this discovery. Both you and Janet will be required to make a very detailed statement. We are going to need to know a lot more about how you came about the information relating to this. Can I use your phone? I need to phone the station."

David had expected this and replied, "Of course you can but can I ask you to be as discreet about this as you possibly can. I don't want to have press and the media and hordes of police investigators milling around the premises and causing distress or questions from our neighbours."

The inspector paused for a few seconds before he spoke.

"David, this is probably going to be a murder investigation based on what you have told me. It's not the sort of thing you can keep under wraps if what you have told me turns out to be true. I'm sorry but I have a duty to the poor unfortunate person who is buried under that concrete and rubble and you can't expect me to hinder any investigation because of any disruption it might cause. I will do my best at this stage until we recover everything from the basement but I can't promise anything."

David thanked the inspector and we all waited. David's brother offered to remain in case his assistance was required to continue further with the excavation work and his colleagues were sent home. We all waited for the police to arrive. I couldn't communicate with Jack or Janet while all this was going on and had to suffer the trauma of my own thoughts and concerns with no one to reassure me or provide guidance. It was a worrying time for me.

The police arrived with forensic specialists and officers with experience of solving murder cases. A detective quickly took control of the situation at the scene. David's brother continued with police guidance to recover my remains. The most harrowing experience for me was the placing of a groundsheet on the office floor and the appearance of my remains being deposited in full view for everyone to see. I had aged well. Unrecognisable. I was stunned and in shock. Janet was distressed and I found out afterwards that it affected Jack too.

The inspector was concerned for Janet and suggested that both Janet and David leave the office keys with him and go home and leave the rest for the police to investigate. Both adamantly refused to leave and the inspector allowed them to remain on the condition that they kept well away from my remains and the work area in the basement.

As dusk approached most of my skeletal remains had been recovered along with various chunks of concrete, debris and fabric in a tangled mess of human remains placed carefully by the police in the right order so as to distinguish the form that was to become a well pieced together skeleton. I admire the skill and dedication of the police and their attention to detail. The amount of effort in cleaning up my physical remains was something I was to witness over the coming days. The most amazing find of all was a gold locket and chain, half-embedded in a lump of concrete and still clutched tightly by the bones of what had been one of my hands. In all the long years since my death I had no idea that I had been in possession of the one piece of evidence that would help lead to the arrest and final conviction of one of my killers. There was no need for a dredger after all.

At this point the proceedings were going to plan and I felt both relieved and concerned at the same time. How I needed to communicate with Janet and Jack now. Janet muttered several comments to me throughout the day in an attempt to reassure me, much to the amusement of the inspector who put it down to the shock and surprise that Janet was experiencing from these traumatic events.

At around 7.30 p.m. events took a turn for the worse. Janet and David were called into one of the offices by the detective whose approach and attitude might be forgiven considering his suspicions and the source of the evidence with which he had been presented. We had all agreed that we would not provide the police with the details of how we had obtained the information. After all, this would take more explaining than the actual crime. We always knew that Janet could not be blamed for my death, she was too young and therefore beyond suspicion. David on the other hand may have just been old enough to have been involved in some way. The detective was convinced that either Janet or David had some involvement in the actual crime. How could they have known about this and what was the source of the information that they had received?

We always knew that some very difficult questions would be asked by the police. Janet had started to make excuses and commented that the document had arrived anonymously in the post. Thankfully, David had considered this scenario beforehand and my laptop, or perhaps I should say the company laptop, had been locked away in a cupboard out of sight. It contained too much information for prying eyes. It turns out this was an extremely good move, for what happened next was completely unexpected.

The interrogation by the detective was raising some very awkward questions and Janet is not good at being untruthful. She is far from convincing in such a situation. Any detective would have picked up on this and he was giving David and Janet a very hard time. The inspector could have been more helpful. I am convinced he knew what was going on and the type of questions that his detective would be asking. I can however understand why he left this to someone else rather than carry out the enquiry himself and put at risk his long-term friendship with David.

Both Jack and I had moved closer to Janet. Something we have always tended to do when she is in distress or is concerned about anything. She knows this and can sense it. Unfortunately things were starting to take a more sinister line of enquiry. The inspector was making veiled threats that if he didn't have more substantial and plausible reasons for how the information had been obtained, he may have to detain either David, Janet, or both of them. References were made to the serious nature of withholding evidence from the police. It was all starting to get out of hand.

The detective was becoming impatient. Janet was looking extremely uncomfortable. I felt so sorry for her and angry at the way the interrogation was progressing. The consequences of a single statement can lead to the most unusual of actions. It was not planned. What happened next should never have happened. It was not our intention from the start. The detective cast an accusing glare at Janet. He was playing on her weakness.

Detective: "Janet, you are lying to me. At the very least you are not telling me the truth. You are leaving me with no alternative than to ask you both to accompany me to the station for a formal interview."

David later reflects on this as 'the moment the shit hit the fan'. This amused me greatly and is a constant topic of discussion between Jack and I when we reflect on what happened. At the time I was very angry with Jack, but what has happened has come to pass.

The detective was studying Janet's reaction and waiting for her answer. The answer he got was completely unexpected. David's electronic personal organiser rose slowly from the desk, seemingly of its own accord. The detective froze motionless in his chair, all confidence and bravado gone now. This was the first time David had witnessed Jack's abilities and even he looked petrified. The organiser moved slowly toward the detective, hovering just inches from his face. A message began to appear on the digital display.

Hello Asshole

After about ten seconds it gracefully reversed and glided to its original resting place on the desk. The shit really had hit the fan. The detective stood up with amazing speed knocking his chair violently to the ground in the process. Without a spoken word he ran out of the room muttering and mumbling under his breath and headed straight for the inspector. I later debated this with Jack who is not known for using such words. I accused him of amateur dramatics and asked him where he had picked up the phrase 'asshole'. Good old Arnie Schwarzenneger had obviously impressed Jack sufficiently with his *Terminator* film that we had recently watched on television over the Christmas break.

The problem is, that had Jack had stopped right there, we might have been able to retrieve the situation and deal with matters more calmly without drawing any attention to ourselves. But no, Jack just had to take things to the extreme. The words 'paper chase' take on a new meaning when you see the contents of an office in-tray project themselves across a room and start wandering around aimlessly amongst police officers and all who are present. I remember thinking at the time that there would be no stopping this and that our very existence was now under threat. I wish I could have communicated with Jack but with all these people present and with the absence of the laptop, that would have been most difficult. Indeed, what followed turned out to be highly interesting and in many ways, most entertaining.

The inspector had stood watching events unfold with disbelief. Everyone had stopped work. The detective was standing behind the inspector as if to screen himself from danger. The inspector made a phone call and announced that no one was to leave the premises. We waited in suspense.

From that point onwards, any fear that we had of media coverage was of little relevance. The police were astonished and at loss to explain what they had just witnessed. It was another two hours before the first of them arrived. Officials in dark business suits from Cheltenham, followed by two individuals from London and rather a strange character from the special investigations unit of the Ministry of Defence. All of them were subjected to an awe inspiring demonstration of Jack's skills. Throughout the night they remained observing this strange phenomena. Equipment was discretely brought into the building and an array of electronic gadgets and radio devices were set up. It was a long night.

On Sunday a high ranking official from the Ministry of Defence arrived with an colleague from the Royal Signals. Everyone present, including Janet and David, was asked to sign the Official Secrets Act. We also heard the inspector talking about a D notice no longer being necessary whilst he was on the phone to a superior at West Midlands Police Headquarters.

So you see, we have had quite an eventful time. The full ramifications of this are not yet resolved. Our daily pattern of existence continues. My burial will take place at some time in the near future. The authorities continue their investigations with bewilderment and intrigue.

To the enquiring mind I leave you with a thought. What if my name is not really Michael Pennington and that there is no Janet and David? What if I have mislead you in order to conceal my real identity and those who are dear to me? What if this took place some months ago. Have you thought that we may actually be in Smethwick or Warley. There are many canals in Birmingham. There are some things that must remain private. I am sure that you will appreciate this.

What I have told you may be false or it may be true. For my part, I exist. My quest and my search continues. There is much to do. Look out for me. The seeker will one day find what they desire. I shall travel the world wide web and continue to locate the lost souls that exist in limbo for as long as I am able to do so. I do not know what the future holds.

Since that eventful day we have been busy working away at our project. My own circumstances and the discovery of my physical remains have caused more than a little upheaval. The situation is now under control and we are documented in great detail within certain government institutions. I hope this provides them with a little insight into what the future holds. They are most certainly in for a big surprise.

My memoirs are written by way of introduction and in order that you may understand the workings and intricacies of the spirit world. Many of you do not believe, and cannot be expected to believe, the content of my memoirs. I have no issue with this. It is the wider implications of my mission that are of interest to me. I write now with concern and with caution. I am unsure how to begin. First, I will provide you with an explanation and a word of warning. What I am about to reveal to you will take you on a journey into another dimension far more overwhelming and unbelievable than my simple existence. It is the very essence of our mission on earth as spirits. It may explain why so many are trapped here on earth and working together towards a common goal and a harmonic existence with the living. This much I now know.

You have all been part of the unfolding story of life on our planet and its future. You are the new 'Pilgrim Fathers' of the revolution that will take place. You are the testing ground. All this did not start with me or with my death but actually began in the late 1980s with the introduction of computers and the internet. There is just so much to tell. My own story is of little relevance but essential in obtaining your consent and interest for my continuation. If you find my writings disturbing you should leave, as to continue may cause you undue stress, and is unlikely to be of any benefit to you.

Whether a person believes or does not believe is of little consequence as this can be proven later. We do not seek to prove or verify our own existence. The time is not right. The world is not ready for us yet.

I, and many others like me, have, and are continually, working the message forums around the globe in preparation. This is an experiment. Whether you are ready or not to accept the possibility or to consider what the future may hold is a matter for you, and you alone, as individuals. Your reactions and observations will decide the outcome of the way in which future contact is made.

I notice that I have been caught out on more than one occasion with my memoirs. The internet is indeed not so large as might be expected. There are a number of variations of my story and many other unique stories that are being used in other forums on the internet and all for the same purpose. Some will be found by you, and others will not. The aim is the same in each case. Humans and spirits are being drawn together as never before. The bonding between the dead and the living is growing. The lost souls are being found and located in ever increasing numbers. There is a growing army of dedicated individuals who are now working towards integration. This is being done with a degree of secrecy. The human idea that spirits have a desire to move on and are troubled and in transit is a myth. We have no influence over this phenomena and we struggle to understand why some are chosen to remain and why others move on. Whilst this may have been true in times gone by this is no longer an ambition for all of us. There are much more wider implications as you will see.

In order for you to understand the reasoning behind this strange method of approach I would request that you consider why the spirit world is not making more of an effort to come forward and claim its rightful place in our destiny. I have touched on this previously. It is not in the human nature to believe in the supernatural and whilst there are many believers, there are many more doubters. Our numbers are not sufficient yet to provide the necessary infrastructure and final proof that you all so desire, and indeed deserve. This day will come, and mankind will discover, beyond any reasonable doubt, that the human race, and life as you know it, has much wider and far reaching implications for you than events and history has provided you with up until now.

Many questions remain unanswered for you. I can understand your frustrations. There are delicate reasons why this has to be. Prepare yourselves for a journey into your future. It is time to move on to a new dimension. Are you really ready?

First Contact

This world is full of intrigue and mysticism. Humans fall into various categories in their ideas, beliefs and fantasies. And then there is religion. Some people believe in aliens and UFOs. There are crop circles and thousands of unexplored and unexplained phenomena. There are ghosts and spirits, demons and vampires, and all manner of strange tales of monsters and myths of legend. This has been apparent since records began. Just why is this so? Is all of this the subject of human imagination or is there more to it than we really think?

Jules Verne once wrote of an imaginary submarine with doors made of neither wood nor metal. This was before submarines or plastic was invented. Who designed a helicopter and a tank over four hundred years before they came into general use? The Inventions of Leonardo da Vinci of course. But how did he know of such things? What of *Star Trek* and the sci-fi films that are watched with enthusiasm around the world. Is this what the future holds for us?

It will come as a surprise to you in that I can inform you that I already know what the future holds for our kind. I am going to tell you a story, let us say an imaginary event that will take place sometime in the next ten years but is very much imbedded in the present.

All across the world, global communications and computers govern every aspect of daily life on planet Earth. Technology continues to move at an ever increasing pace and the advent of nanotechnology is in its infancy. Cloning is also in its early stages and the day-to-day life of the average human is one of a constant battle and an emotional roller coaster of work, leisure, family relations, daily stress, and in some cases, for some humans, a traumatic and miserable existence.

Television, holidays, digital media, books, sport and a host of creature comforts ensure that life is more than bearable for the majority of humans in the Western World. People continue to struggle with their obsession for wealth and improvement. Life is fragile and governed by laws and institutions that ensure an organised and structured existence for most of the human race.

Terrorism continues to cause strife and remains a constant excuse for war and retribution. The religions and their spokespersons on earth can find no words or acts that constrain the tide of hate and distrust between nations. Rogue states continue to act outside of what is regarded and commonly accepted as International Law.

Life continues in much the same way as it always has done. Improvement and advances in technology ensure that the human race makes progress. Faster communications and the common acceptance of computers as an essential household item ensure that our destiny is absolute. Most homes will have a broadband or ADSL connection and use of the internet has become a way of life and an accepted method of communication globally. Even poor homes and small villages in distant lands can find access to a computer connected to the internet.

Across the world something exciting is happening. Word is spreading of strange contacts and stories on message forums. So-called weirdos claiming to be spirits and ghosts are providing accounts of what life or existence has been like for them. Almost every country in the world is experiencing unbelievable tales of supernatural experiences that can neither be proven or denied. What if some of these stories were true?

Disturbing accounts of a presence or spirits in government departments around the globe are starting to increase at an alarming rate. In the past, human fascination with UFOs and alien beings from other planets have caused a limited degree of hysteria and concern to the authorities but have always been dismissed as supposition. There has never been any hard evidence. Not tangible evidence or confirmation beyond reasonable doubt. Somehow this is different. Reports are coming in from responsible citizens from almost every nation describing strange encounters with unusual people in chat rooms and forums who are describing their past lives and accounts of experiences that pertain to the supernatural. They claim they are the living dead. Concerns are being expressed in the media that a global cult or new religion is behind the spreading of such rumours, and governments continue to provide their citizens with little or no information on the subject. Life is about to change for planet Earth.

Preparations are being made for an extraordinary encounter. A true undeniable test for the human race is in the making. It happens in the not too distant future and begins as a normal and uneventful day with regard to world news. However, by the close of day, every communication channel available to mankind will be the subject of one topic alone and other world news will pale into insignificance.

Recent reports by individuals claiming to be involved in communication with the spirit world have provided a message. One message. It is always the same message. There are thousands and thousands of unconfirmed reports that a sign will be provided to formally introduce the existence of the afterlife to all citizens of our planet. Television and media programs have investigated these claims but nothing has been proven. For some reason the spirits seem to be coordinating a timed event. There is no proof but it cannot be denied that the numbers involved are beyond comprehension.

It is mid July and a bright and cheerful day in Washington DC. The hustle and bustle of daily life is what you would expect for a rush hour Monday morning. Office workers arriving for work, traffic congestion, shoppers and strollers going about their day-to day-business. A normal and uneventful day by all accounts.

At exactly 9.00 a.m. it happens. Without warning, without any announcement, there is a power failure. Lights across the city fail instantly. Traffic lights cease to operate. Office blocks are plunged into darkness. Elevators fail. All communication by radio, satellite and television ceases.

Robert Haskell is a computer analyst with a large insurance company and is sat by his desk in the middle of a conversation with the actuaries when the phone line goes dead and the lights in the office go out. Robert's cubicle is one of many and he stands to observe the look on the faces of his colleagues as they shuffle around in the half light.

He is calm and collected and he waits patiently. There are over a hundred people in this open-plan office. Each with a cubicle. Each with a computer.

The computer monitors burst into life, flicker and glow. Most unusual considering the lights are still off and the computer units do not appear to be operating. For a few seconds nothing happens. As if by magic the words mysteriously appear from nowhere and, like the sub titles on a film, they arrange themselves neatly in the centre of the screen. The background is black. The letters are white. The message reads;

Greetings from the Spirit World

For a full minute the message remains on the monitors. The lights come on, elevators spring back to life and communications are working again. The message has gone, computers are rebooting and everything is returning to normal. Normal? The look and the expressions on people's faces are confirmation that what has just happened is anything but normal. Robert sat back in his chair and smiled. At last, having dedicated so much of his spare time in the last five years to the cause, he could now prepare for what was to come. It had finally come to pass. All the effort, the frustration and the personal cost would be worthwhile. Life would never be the same again. Had anyone been watching they would have been concerned, but he was used to covering his tracks and being careful. He looked to his right and smiled again.

"Looks like were going to be busy, Maggie," he said.

The word document opened on his computer and the writing appeared.

Maggie: Sure thing Rob, so glad that I got you around, I reckon I need as much help as these guys are going to need to get through what comes next.

"That's for sure," said Robert.

With that he reached for his Lucky Strike cigarettes. It was a non-smoking office but he had no concerns. He took out his Zippo lighter and lit his cigarette, inhaling deeply with the first draw. A colleague to his right noticed him lighting up and gave an enquiring look.

"Hey, Charlie, at times like this, who gives a shit," he said nonchalantly.

The phones never stopped that day. No work was done. Some people panicked and went home. Others were convinced that they had just experienced a global virus of some kind. There were many theories and guesses. All across the USA the same event had been experienced by millions of people, at exactly the same time, in exactly the same manner and in every habitable corner of the country.

Normal television broadcasts were interrupted with improvised news bulletins. Within half an hour the president of the United States was on television and looked about as convincing as the local street vendor with his theories and possible causes for what had just transpired. A plea for calm and reasoning was the theme of the day but it did not stop the declaring of a national state of emergency or the calling out of the National Guard to ensure that law and order was retained.

It was not unique to the USA. The same thing occurred in every country across the entire globe. Governments were in constant contact with their allies and searching for answers and a logical explanation for what had happened. Old enemies and despots from third world countries cast aside their differences and political agendas in a desperate attempt to obtain information and a cohesive solution to what they could not understand. They would not have long to wait. There would be a planned interlude and cessation of activity while the final preparations were being made.

Before you enquire as to how it could be possible for mere spirits to organise and plan such an event or physically carry out such an amazing task, I would respectfully request that you refrain from theory and logic and possible solutions and causes. It is not an event that can be explained by physics, the laws of nature or the world as you currently know it. All will be revealed in the future.

I have to say that our government in the UK and similarly the USA and Canada have provided no detailed report or professional explanation for the recent power cuts experienced in our countries. National Grid said an 'oversensitive automatic protection relay' shut off supplies to three power stations on 28 August 2003, leaving 410,000 homes and businesses without electricity and paralysing the Underground and train services.

And what of the USA and Canada? The power failures caused chaos as they spread from New York to Detroit, and Toronto to Ottawa. Traffic lights failed, underground railways were evacuated and people were trapped in lifts in offices and apartments.

Canadian officials said a fire at a power plant near the upstate New York town of Niagara caused the outage, but US officials disputed that theory, although they said terrorism was not to blame.

How interesting that the US and Canadian authorities have conflicting stories. Why do they not provide detailed and statistical evidence for such a large disruption? Just why are they blaming each other and providing no answers? The real reason is that they do not know what the cause was. Furthermore, you can expect much more of this in the near future. The testing and preparation has only recently begun.

Whilst Jack and I have struggled to come to terms with our situation and have now met many others around the world who are dedicated to the cause, our transition into this new and exciting way of existence has not been easy. I have had to contend with my remains being excavated and with the weary investigations that have taken place at our premises in Oldbury. Janet and David have not had an easy time of it either.

Why did we decide to tell our story to you? I know many of you have been wondering just what is the point of the whole exercise. Only now are you beginning to find out why. Our network grows daily and the success of this network will depend on the number of humans and spirits that can work together side by side in order to provide the welcoming and the integration for the future benefit of mankind and its understanding of the afterlife.

Things have moved on. What we have started here now is the method by which we shall try and establish a foundation for the future communication between humans and the supernatural. The quicker we can organise this event the better for all concerned. We have no wish to see the current situation continue at the slow pace it has since the early 1980s. It is time to test the water and step up a gear or two. I have finally managed to convince others that this is the way forward.

In key locations around the globe our infrastructure is being meticulously pieced together. We have spirits and humans in key government locations. We have office workers, drivers, managers, housewives, military personnel and a host of other professions and capabilities at our disposal. I hope this does not sound in any way sinister. It is not intentional. The first step is to involve people, not governments or the sceptical press or those looking for personal gain. Our mission needs people and, as you know, it also needs more of the lost souls that are still out there. There are many who are trapped as a result of the traumatic experiences of their past. To resolve this issue will require a consolidated effort from both the living and the spirits of our world.

For some, the possibilities may seem far-fetched, but you may at least have an open mind. For many of you this is a subject that will become more meaningful in later years as our mission progresses and becomes more well known and widespread. The day of reckoning and reconciliation draws ever closer to becoming a reality.

The Investigation Continues

The continuing investigation and subsequent visits by the inspector and his conversations with Janet and David continued to provided us with more intriguing details and as events unfolded we were able to piece together the full details of the crime that cut my life short back in 1971.

The research had taken on a clandestine approach and was treated with caution and presented the police with many difficulties. The absence of any real living witness was making progress difficult. The police were aware of the need for more evidence and some hard facts in order to bring the case to a close.

The inspector had become a confirmed believer and Jack and I would listen to many conversations and theories exchanged in conversations between David, Janet and the inspector. After a period of three weeks the police had unearthed some interesting facts regarding George Roberts, the second and unwitting accomplice in my murder case. The inspector was determined to bring the case to a successful conclusion and called round one Thursday afternoon with this interesting and new information. Janet and David, accompanied by Jack and I listened with great interest as the inspector revealed his findings as they sat in David's office that rainy afternoon.

"I've got some interesting information that I would like your thoughts on," the inspector said, in a slow and deliberate manner. "The second man in your account of Michael's death was a Mr George Roberts, a builder by trade and a working colleague of Clive Mellows. We have information about Clive Mellows that could possibly lead to the opening of a fresh murder case. This is something that was not investigated at the time but is now of more relevance in light of the information regarding Michael."

The inspector went on to describe the details of the death of George. It transpired that just one week after my murder, George had fallen from scaffolding on a building project that Clive Mellows' firm had been involved with in nearby Smethwick. The renovation of this particular property involved the conversion of a small ceramic factory to residential flats. Details of the coroner's report clearly stated accidental death by injuries sustained from falling from scaffolding whilst working on the building's roof. Our inspector now had reason to believe that George Roberts' death might be in some way connected with my own murder. Proving such a case would be difficult. There was a distinct lack of evidence and no means by which any criminal involvement could be established.

Jack and I were astounded and the look on Janet and David's faces confirmed that they too were at a loss for any rational explanation. The inspector continued with his theory.

"Let's assume that the two builders argued about Michael's death after they left the scene. Possibly George was traumatised by the murder and wanted to come clean and go to the police. We cannot rule out the possibility that Clive may have killed George in order to keep him quiet. I am struggling for a way to bring this case to a close but I have no evidence to convict Clive Mellows other than the discovery of his locket and your account which would be difficult to substantiate in a court of law. I am turning to you for help and assistance as I have an idea that our friends Jack and Michael may be able to assist us further in our investigations."

The inspector continued. "This is a remote possibility, but let's just suppose that Jack or Michael were able to establish contact with George. After all, he has suffered a violent death and his spirit might still be present at the building in Smethwick. If you could in some way provide an account of what happened it might enable us to piece together the final part of the jigsaw and assist us in providing enough evidence to Clive in order to obtain his signed confession."

This new information was of great concern to Jack and I. Janet and David struggled to work out the logistics of making contact with another spirit in a different location and the intricate details of how any such contact might develop and how it might be of use in solving my murder.

The inspector was worried and concerned for Janet in asking for her assistance and told us about a medium that he had dealings with whilst working for the police. We listened intently as the inspector described Stephen, a medium who had an amazing gift and who had unofficially been used by the police to help piece together certain crime mysteries in the past. We had no idea that the police used such people but Stephen was certainly a very gifted person as we were soon to find out.

It was agreed that David and Janet would meet Stephen and seek his assistance and experience in helping to resolve this crime. We waited in anticipation of his arrival.

Stephen is forty-two years old but looks older and is almost bald. A gaunt individual, quite scruffy in appearance he works for the local council in the planning department. Stephen is not the type of person that you would associate with being a medium and has no interest in using his gift for commercial gain or advantage.

There have been many occasions when Stephen has experienced strange dreams which he refers to as flashbacks. He has no understanding of how this works but is often able to recall events from suicide victims or dreams about crimes, violent deaths and locations that have resulted in the police being able to piece together information that would not have been freely available without assistance from Stephen.

Stephen has possessed this gift from early childhood and his first experience with assisting the police almost led to his arrest. Understandably the police were very sceptical but over the years they have become accustomed to his strange forecasts and are more than willing to consider any information that he provides. Stephen is not alone in this respect. There are other accounts of similar cases in the UK. The details of flashbacks are not accepted as evidence in court but they are extremely useful in leading the police to investigate certain crimes and save the police a lot of frustration and investigative work. This is all carried out unofficially and without reference to the source of the information in any documentation.

The inspector was also able to confirm that Stephen claimed to be in contact with the spirit world. No longer a sceptic, our inspector made it quite clear that Stephen could be a very useful ally and a powerful tool in our search for George. This would also assist Janet and provide her with a welcome accomplice in her efforts to establish contact with George.

When Stephen first arrived at our offices in Oldbury he was immediately conscious of our presence. Our first impressions were of a rather odd individual of quiet disposition who is softly spoken and with a nervous attitude that did not inspire us with confidence on our first encounter. How wrong our assumption proved to be and became very evident as matters progressed.

After lengthy discussion with the inspector, Janet and David laboriously and painstakingly explained the full details of our existence and the amazing account of our life and the events that had taken place, whilst Stephen listened with interest and without any visible expression of disbelief or belief.

What he was about to reveal gave Jack and I much cause for alarm and concern with regard to our own plight. When Stephen finally spoke he provided us with information that helped confirm one of the possible reasons for our presence and our mission here on earth.

"I can feel a presence here with us in this very room," Stephen said. "It is a strong presence and I have no reason to doubt that what you say is true. You see, I have for a number of years now been in contact with the spirit world by computer. I have several friends who are aware of Michael and Jack and their existence has been made known to me through various postings around the internet and from personal contacts both living and dead. I am a firm believer of the supernatural and pride myself in being a member of this growing community of spirits and humans who are seeking redemption for the lost souls that exist and who are waiting for their chance to move on. I have helped many in this situation which has become a personal crusade for me and a mission which I regard of such high importance that it has become my life's work."

Jack and I were astounded. We hung on Stephen's every word. So this was what it was all about? I was filled with a sense of fear and panic as Stephen continued. I was all the more surprised when he looked towards Jack and I and appeared to be addressing us personally as he continued.

"There is nothing for you to fear. As far as I am able to determine, the reason you exist as spirits is based on your mission to ensure that the wrongdoings of the past are brought to account. Jack is an integral part of this mission and his reason for not moving on is based on the fact that his work in assisting Michael is not yet finished. I do not claim to have the answers as to why he waited almost fifty years to experience Michael's death but I do know of similar instances where this phenomenon is present. This is not an isolated case. There are many such cases. It would seem that there are thousands of others drawn together for a variety of purposes that we are unable to fully understand and that there are many unexplained reasons behind the existence of the afterlife. In the future I am sure that we will all have a better understanding as to the reasons why such phenomena exist. For now we are but a small group of individuals struggling to comprehend the details and the logic that defies all known laws of physics as we understand them."

Meeting Stephen and his rational explanation was in some ways a source of comfort to Jack and I. It was all beginning to make more sense. We would now turn our attentions toward the task in hand and devote our efforts towards finding George. This was no simple matter and would require a great deal of preparation and planning.

Over the coming days, Jack and I would discuss Stephen's information and revelations time and time again in order to try and understand the purpose of our very existence and debate the implications of moving on and what it might mean for us. We had no answers and our theories were of supposition rather than based on any material evidence or facts.

David, Janet and Stephen, with helpful input and information from the inspector, struggled with detailed plans and preparations for establishing contact with George. How would I react if I met George? Would I ever meet George? How would this all end? I had more questions than I had answers at this time.

The Ghost Walk

Based on our experience with Jack, Janet had planned a visit to the converted flats in Smethwick. She would be accompanied by Stephen and use the same approach as she had when first contact with Jack was established. This time it would prove to be more difficult.

By studying the A-Z map of Oldbury and Smethwick we could determine that the building where George had died was just over a mile and a half from our own location in Oldbury. It was also very close to the canal. By careful planning we were able to trace a quiet route by following the canal path towards Smethwick, passing through an industrial estate to the quiet cul-de-sac where the residential building was situated. We had no idea if it would be possible to bring George over such a long distance to our location here in Oldbury. We were about to find out.

It was decided that Janet and Stephen would leave the offices at 4 p.m. on a Friday night. Reconnaissance of the flats had resulted in establishing contact with an amused occupant who was quite helpful and intrigued as to the appearance of two Ghost Hunters from a local Ghost Hunting Club. Emma had kindly offered to let her strange visitors into the complex and give them a guided tour. Emma did not believe in the supernatural but looked on the situation as the means of some light entertainment before going out for a drink with her friends.

When Janet and Stephen arrived she was most hospitable and provided a welcome cup of tea and biscuits for her guests. The building consisted of twelve separate apartments and a central staircase with access to the roof and basement area which was used as storage and for which Emma had a key.

Janet left the embarrassing details and explanations to Stephen who was most adept at reassuring Emma that they were convinced of the presence of a friendly ghost in the vicinity of the apartments and that their investigation was just a matter of routine and of local interest. Emma was relaxed in their company and her initial concerns about the pair were put at ease with both Janet and Stephen providing her with proof of their identity and details of their ghost hunting hobby.

Emma was quite happy to let Janet and Stephen take a look around the building and observed their monitoring from a distance with a bemused look and a concentrated effort to resist the urge to burst out giggling at the couple's strange antics. Emma had to leave them temporarily to avoid embarrassment when they promptly produced an A4 piece of paper with bold type and held it in the air for an imaginary person to read. They carried out this exercise several times and from a variety of locations. Emma thought it was hilarious and that it would make a good story to tell when she arrived at her local pub. When she overheard Stephen confirming that he could feel a presence she wondered why two seemingly down-to-earth and sensible individuals would have such a strange and cranky hobby.

Stephen gives a rather different account. This is recalled and documented in his own words:

When I entered the building I immediately became aware of a presence. It was almost as if we were being followed. Emma has a small and neatly-kept one bedroomed flat on the ground floor. The presence was able to move around the building with ease. I held up our typed document several times in order to make sure that our message was understood. The content of that message was as follows:

Message for George Roberts

George. We hope that you can read this. We know you are here. We think that you have been the victim of a terrible crime which dates back to 1971.

The reason you are still here is unclear to us although we think we may have the answer. It is thought that you might be able to leave this building and accompany us to another location. It is over a mile and a half away. If you can do this we may be able to help you and others who are in the same situation as you.

We have a spirit friend who is able to communicate with us by using a computer. His email address is michaelpennington1971@yahoo.co.uk. If you are able to use a computer you can contact him at this address. It would be advantageous if you could follow us as we would like you to meet him.

Please help us to assist you and try and follow us. We mean you no harm and only wish to help you.

Stephen and Janet.

We thanked Emma for her hospitality and left the building. The moment the door closed we realised that the presence either could not or was unwilling to follow. We were alone again. We made our way back to the office in Oldbury, disappointed that our mission had been a failure.

When Janet and Stephen returned, David and the inspector were waiting impatiently along with Jack and I and we were bitterly disappointed that the contact had not resulted in establishing any communication with George. I suppose this was understandable, given the fact that George would probably have recognised my name and would have been fearful of a meeting with his victim. In hindsight we all agreed that this had been a fatal flaw in our plans to establish a dialogue with George.

For the next two weeks events proceeded rather slowly. Regular visits from the inspector brought no new evidence and my case remained open. We had achieved so much in such a short space of time and yet we were now at a loss as to what course of action to take. It seemed as if we were destined to remain in a state of limbo and unable to fulfil our mission. We had almost become accustomed to the idea that we would not after all be able to provide a satisfactory conclusion to our investigation.

David and Janet were busy planning another visit to the flats and Stephen had arrived to help with the plans in what would be our final attempt to establish contact with George. Whilst they fussed around making coffee and chatting, Jack and I communicated with each other by way of our open word document and I checked my email. There it was. I had mail. I had an email from George Roberts. Excitedly, Jack casually tossed a pencil at Janet to attract her attention and everyone rushed to the laptop to read the email. We were absolutely astonished as we read the content.

From: GeorgeRoberts
To: MichaelPennington1971@yahoo.co.uk
Subject: Hello

Dear Michael, Janet and Stephen,

I have been following the internet and learning about computers for some time. I have also read your postings on the internet. I am deeply ashamed and worried about responding to your visit and cannot express how sad and troubled I have been by recent events. I did not try and follow you as you requested as I have no idea what to expect or what can be gained by meeting up with Michael.

I have been condemned to an existence that is worse than any prison could be, trapped with my thoughts and frustrations over the years. I am sure Michael understands what this must be like. I have no human friends. I observe the world from my prison, and from my borrowed internet connection, which at least gives me a sense of purpose and hope for the future.

Your visit was deeply shocking and frightening and yet I cannot ignore your request which I think about constantly each day and night. How can Michael ever forgive me? Just what can I say or do that will redeem me or provide me with some salvation and end the misery of my past from which I cannot escape.

There is so much I yearn to tell and yet I cannot bring myself to face the consequences of my actions all those years long ago. If I could turn back the clock I would truly do so. This is of course not possible. If it is any consolation I can confirm that I suffered a similar fate to Michael by the hands of the same Clive Mellows.

I would beg your forgiveness of me and I understand that I have no right to expect your pity or your blessing or any form of redemption for my sins. I cannot begin to express the sorrow, the sadness or the anger that has been with me since my death.

George Roberts.

I must have read that message a hundred times. The inspector had been correct in his assumptions. It is difficult to portray the mixed feelings and resentment, intermingled with pity, and, at the same time anger, that such a communication delivers to a reader and victim such as myself.

We discussed the implications of George's communication. Stephen convinced us to try once more to persuade George that the best course of action was one of reconciliation and forgiveness that would assist all of us towards a common goal. I logged into my Yahoo account and thoughtfully constructed my reply. I needed to convince George that however I may have felt, the only course of action now open to us was one of introduction and cooperation in order to fulfil our destiny and our journey to our final resting place. It took a long time and many corrections before the final email I eventually sent to George. Janet cried when she read its content. Stephen and David sat solemnly and seemingly rooted to their seats as I hit the send button on my final draft to George.

Dear George,

Thank you for your email. I will not lie to you and say that I find forgiving your actions an easy task. I think that this is something that we can discuss and I am sure that you have more to tell us about the person who placed us in our current predicament.

The fact that you are also the victim of the very same person who caused my death all those years ago does confirm that at least you had more concern and guilt than our murderer. You have suffered the same unfortunate fate, and in that I can relate to you and your current situation.

If nothing else, and no matter how hard this may be for you, I feel that the very least you owe me is the pleasure of your acquaintance. This would appear to be in both of our interests. I am sure you seek retribution and justice against Clive in the same way as I do. My anger and my wish for vengeance cannot be mine alone. You too must share these feelings.

Let us try and resolve this issue and cooperate towards what must be our joint purpose and very reason for our continued existence as spirits in the living world.

Yours truly,
Michael Pennington

Our loyal human friends prepared once more to visit George, and Stephen expressed his confidence that George would now comply with our request. During the final preparations I made my decision to accompany them and to visit George personally. I had no idea how hard this might be or whether I might end up trapped in some other location or lost to the world between Oldbury and Smethwick. I just had to do this. I dared not leave things to chance. I would rely on my association with Janet and Stephen to get me through, and I had every confidence that they would be able detect and track my whereabouts, and that I would not be left alone in some desolate place to wander around aimlessly for eternity. When the time came I was ready. I had emailed George and we had exchanged several communications. I had actually become concerned with his plight, as indeed, I was for my own.

This was not the first time I had left the offices of course. The difference was the distance involved. It was certainly a walk into the unknown. Both Stephen and Janet walked slowly and were constantly reassuring each other that they could still feel my presence. It would have been a strange sight for any observer, two people walking along the canal side, muttering and exchanging comments as they looked around for an imaginary child or person that no one else would have seen.

As we walked along the canal path I observed the many buildings and heard the sights and sounds I had missed since being alive. It was all new territory for me and I was captivated by the surroundings as a child might be with a new toy or a good film. It occurred to me that I should have tried this before and ventured out more. We finally arrived at our destination.

As we approached the entrance I became nervous and paranoid and only Janet's soothing and reassuring voice spurred me to take those last few steps to the entrance. I waited for Stephen to ring the doorbell of Emma's flat but the door was open as if someone had been expecting our arrival. As we entered the foyer I instantly knew that George was with us. I experienced the same feeling I got when I first collided with Jack. That gut-wrenching searing sensation and blinding light is something I have never become accustomed to, and it catches me by surprise each time it happens. I could just make out the aura of George as I positioned myself to one side and let Stephen do the introduction.

"Hello George. Michael is with us. He is not angry and you know he bears no malice. Michael has managed to come this far which means that you should be able to accompany us back to our offices in Oldbury where our other spirit friend Jack is also waiting to meet you. There is a computer waiting and we hope that the three of you can become acquainted and get to know each other. Please try and follow us back. We do really want to resolve this situation. I am positive that we can work things out."

As we left the flats I collided with George once again. He was with us at last and the journey back to Oldbury was uneventful and without trauma. Stephen and Janet babbled incessantly and uttered words of reassurance along the whole route. It was difficult for them to know what to say. Holding a conversation without answers or acknowledgement cannot be an easy task. They were wonderful.

Finally, there we were, three spirits and four humans. Janet, Stephen, David, the inspector and George, Jack and I, all six of us huddled around a laptop. What a strange sight. In time we would come to respect George. What he told us allowed me to come to terms with my situation and to understand his. A rapid exchange of words ensued and we exchanged greetings via an open word document on the laptop. George had years of pent-up frustrations to deal with, and with no one to listen to his troubles until now, he wasted no time in detailing his account of what had happened all those years ago.

We all sat there and watched as George told his amazing story. Our destiny and our future was rapidly drawing to its conclusion and I remember thinking that my days on earth were numbered.

George: Michael I am going to tell you what happened exactly as events took place.

I worked with Clive Mellows for over nine years. The man was a rogue and always in trouble for drinking and fighting at our local pub. Clive was a bad influence on me and got me into various situations and trouble on many occasions and he had a couple of convictions for grievous bodily harm. I never realised the extent of his anger or the consequences of his actions until that fateful day back in March 1971.

What happened to you was inconceivable and should never have taken place. It was a spur of the moment and unprovoked attack. I thought he was joking when he first turned into the boatyard all those years ago and parked the van in the courtyard. He had been drinking and was short of cash. He rambled on about being desperate to get hold of some money quickly and talked about how easy it was to rob someone along the canal banks. I am sure now that he had done this type of thing before but I have no proof of this.

We saw you coming, Michael. We were hidden from sight by the gate at the back of the boatyard. I never thought that things would work out the way they did. I just followed him and have no excuse for my actions or no logical reason why I allowed him to do what he did. I never dreamed that it would result in a murder. I was worried that he had a knife but thought that he was just going to use it to frighten you into handing over your money.

You know what happened. What happened is history and the reason why you are still here. I am sure it's the reason I am still here too and the same goes for Jack. It all happened so fast. When we sped off in the van I was sick all over the place. I couldn't sleep and I couldn't get you out of my mind. The thought of you lying there dying or dead kept coming back like a recurring nightmare. I became disturbed and couldn't concentrate on my work. I was becoming insane with worry and guilt.

On the day of my death I couldn't take it any longer. Clive knew how I felt. I had told him so many times. I should have thought about it more carefully. I should have reported it to the police straight away and just after the event. I was confused and unstable.

Clive had no such concerns. He constantly told me to stop worrying and that if I ever went to the police I would regret it and be an accessory to murder. On the morning of my death we were working on the roof of the building in Smethwick. The weather was bad and it had started to rain.

I was weak and had been unable to eat or drink properly and it was beginning to affect my health. That morning I blurted it all out to Clive as we stopped for a tea break. I told him that I had to report it to the police. He became angry and violent and threatened me with a crowbar, insisting that I promise him that I would never tell a living soul.

When I refused to confirm that I wouldn't tell anyone he wrestled me to the ground and pressed his face close to mine, snarling and shouting that he would rather kill me than go to prison. I managed to break free and started to make my way down the scaffolding. As I looked up I saw a large scaffolding plank careering downwards towards me. It caught me full in the face and I plunged to the ground. The fall broke my back and I remember the sound of my breaking bones clearly to this day. I remember looking up and seeing Clive peering over the scaffolding rail. He overturned a hod of bricks which hurtled through the air and hit my lifeless body. I blacked out. I don't remember much else. When I awoke it was all like a dream. I stood watching as my body was placed in an ambulance. I had to listen to Clive telling the police how I had slipped whilst carrying bricks up the scaffolding and how he had tried to revive me after my fall. I was horrified and sickened at his attitude and the deceitful way in which he explained my death.

I have remained within the confines of that complex ever since, and until today. I had to endure the daily visits of Clive and his team of builders and watch them go about their daily business and observe Clive pretending to be concerned and sad at my death. He was a good actor and very convincing. I have so much hate for him. All I could do was watch him and curse his very existence. When Clive and the builders finally completed the conversion I was alone until the flats were sold.

I have been using computers for over two years. I found I could use a computer quite by chance and from watching the bachelor at flat 8 using his PC to watch porn and surf the internet. I finally learned how to communicate with others when the PC was unattended. The owner suspects nothing. I always covered my tracks and made sure that I remained untraceable.

About two months ago I came across your postings on the internet. I have been traumatised ever since. It brought everything back to me. You have no idea how this feels. When Stephen and Janet paid a visit I was devastated and confused about what course of action I should take.

Now I am here. I am truly sorry for what has happened but please believe me in that I would never have stabbed you or left you in that condition. Clive killed you. I am guilty by association and by not coming forward or contacting the police. I could have called an ambulance or done more. This much I know. I deserve what happened to me. I am repentant and I beg you for forgiveness. I don't know what else to say.

George had stopped typing. I read his words again and had mixed feelings about the situation. I was unsure as to how this new contact with George would help my case and how the inspector would be able to use George's spiritual testimony in the absence of any living witness. The ingenuity of our inspector was about to be put to the test.

Over a period of time we have become accustomed to George. He often sits apart and away from Jack and I and is troubled with his own thoughts and past experience. We have reassured him on many occasions that he has been accepted and I finally forgave him for his part in my murder. This does not prevent him from feeling helpless and we have learned that his true feelings are of resentment and anger towards a certain Mr Clive Mellows. This is understandable and I feel the same way. Our task is now one of retribution and justice.

I have always referred to our dealings with the inspector in purely career terms and without mentioning his name. The omission of his name is intentional but perhaps we should refer to him as Inspector Smith in order to give him a name we can relate to.

Inspector Smith is without doubt a diligent and persistent individual. He prides himself on his past successes and it is obvious that my case has caused him to review and evaluate his entire method of thinking. It has almost become a personal crusade for him to piece together the intricate details of my murder and to bring the culprit to account for his actions.

When Inspector Smith finally called round to evaluate my case and finalise the details leading to the arrest of Mr Mellows, none of us, human or spirit, had any idea as to the devious methods that he would use in order to bring about a successful conclusion. I have to admire his ingenuity and dedication. I suppose this could never have been a straight forward case.

Inspector Smith sat around the table with the rest of us. There we were, the two victims, the witness, David, Janet, Stephen and the inspector. The detective who had born the brunt of Jack's anger on our previous encounter had reluctantly agreed to accompany the inspector on the assurance that there was no 'funny business' as he so aptly put it.

Everyone sat around and mused over the available evidence. My account, Jack's account and that of George's were read over and checked several times. The inspector constantly twitched and chewed at his lip in deep concentration and in an attempt to work out a way in which to present his evidence to Clive Mellors in order to obtain a signed confession. Finally, he sighed and announced the course of action that we would take.

"This case is not going to stand up in court unless we take some drastic action," he said forcefully. "We all know who the guilty party is but we also know the history of Michael's exhumation of his remains and the chaos that followed. This cannot be allowed to be revealed in court or we shall all become a laughing stock. Furthermore, there are parts of this case that now fall under the Official Secrets Act and are the result of ongoing investigations by other government departments.

"It is essential that we all work together and use the available resources that are at our disposal to our best advantage. By that I mean Michael, Jack and George. We will have to bring Mr Mellows here and demonstrate that we have enough hard evidence to put him away for a long time, probably for the rest of his natural life. This requires a rather devious approach, and possibly dishonest methods on our part," he explained.

"This information must be presented in such a way as to give Mr Mellows no option than to declare his guilt in the form of a statement which matches completely the evidence that we have been presented with. There is no room for error. We only have once chance to get this right."

The office became a hive of activity that weekend. Inspector Smith called in forensics and handwriting analysts. A signed testimonial from George relating to his witnessing of a bad traffic accident in 1969 was still on record and in

George's handwriting. The police were about to commit the cardinal sin of fabricating the evidence. What an outrageous plan. But would it work?

Handwriting experts from West Midlands Police painstakingly forged a statement on behalf of George which outlined the circumstances behind his death and appeared to be in his own handwriting and with his own forged signature. The account was graphical and accurate in every detail and included the conversation George had with Clive prior to his sudden death. The document was compiled using a typed form and dated and stamped as it would have been in 1971. The scene was set. Inspector Smith despatched two police officers to arrest Clive Mellors on suspicion of murder. They were instructed to bring him to our offices in Oldbury. At last, after thirty-three years I was to meet my murderer.

The atmosphere in the office was so tense. The inspector was agitated and engrossed in his preparation. Jack and I managed a short exchange away from the prying eyes of the detective and discussed the likely outcome and our possible future if events were to turn out favourably.

When Clive Mellows finally arrived he was a pitiful character whom I despised immediately. I hadn't realised the amount of hate and anger that had built up inside me all those years. Here I was face to face with my killer and I could do nothing but watch and wait as the inspector commenced with his line of interrogation.

This despicable man was obviously uneasy and uncomfortable with his surroundings. Quite rightly so considering he knew the history behind this building and what he thought must still lie secure beneath its foundations.

Clive Mellors was a master of deceit and cunning. His pretentious attitude and querying nature as to why he had been brought to an office in Oldbury was amazing considering the circumstances. I couldn't help but notice his nervous glance towards the gaping hole in the wall that led to the cellar. This must have given him reason for concern as his nervous reaction and change in facial expression registered his fear of what was to come.

In a very matter-of-fact manner, Inspector Smith proceeded to interrogate Clive Mellows. Years of interviewing had taught him to remain expressionless and unemotional as he reeled out the details of Jack's account of my death. Clive Mellows sat in stunned silence and astonishment as the inspector recounted the conversation word for word that had taken place between him and George all those years ago.

Clive Mellors wasted no time in reminding the inspector of his rights, and immediately requested a solicitor. The inspector explained that a solicitor would be provided and that this was a preliminary investigation at this stage. Mr Mellors looked slightly relieved at the inspector's comment, that is, until he was presented with the signed document with George's signature. The inspector read the statement out to Clive Mellows as he sat ashen-faced and in stunned silence.

Clive Mellows leapt out of the chair in a panic. He started shouting and waving his arms about in a distressed manner.

"That's impossible, I remember exactly what happened. He fell of the scaffolding and he was dead when the ambulance arrived. No way is that statement his. Where did you get that? This can't be happening, this isn't true," he said.

"Mr Mellows," the inspector calmly explained, "There is something you need to know. George Roberts was taken to hospital in a coma and was indeed pronounced dead on arrival. What you are unaware of is that to the surprise of the doctors and medical staff, he made a short recovery whilst he was in hospital. We took his statement at the time and would have arrested you but for lack of evidence. New evidence has now come to light that indicates without a shred of doubt that you were indeed here at this boatyard in 1971 and that you murdered a man called Michael Pennington.

"You see, whilst George gave a brief statement of the circumstances surrounding his death, he was unable to give us the exact location of the scene of the murder of Michael Pennington. He was after all dying and probably did not wish to reveal his part in this ugly crime. However, we have since located a body. I think you know where that body is situated. Do you recognise this?"

The inspector produced a gold locket and put it face down on the table. Clive Mellows was horrified and slumped back in his chair with an air of defeat. Everyone in the room thought that Clive Mellows would now sign a statement admitting his crime. We were wrong. Clive Mellows suddenly regained his composure.

"I demand a solicitor. I'm not guilty and I am saying nothing until I get a solicitor. I don't know where you got this information from but it's all lies and I want to know what witnesses you have. I think it's all guesswork," he sneered at the inspector.

The inspector smiled. Everyone else looked defeated. The inspector had one last ace up his sleeve. It was something that none of us had anticipated but the inspector was determined to obtain a confession. He had already crossed the boundaries of what was legally acceptable and was resigned to the fact that he might be facing early retirement and a disgraceful end to his exemplary career to date.

The inspector had planned this all along. What was unexpected was the way in which he addressed Mr Mellows. The results were nothing short of spectacular.

"Mr Mellows," he said, "Do you believe in the supernatural?"

"Don't be so bloody stupid – what do you take me for?" Clive replied.

The inspector dismissed the detective and closed the door. His words and the chilling manner with which he delivered his next statement would have frightened any living soul.

"I take you for what you are, Clive Mellows," he said, "A lying, deceitful, low life of a human being that murdered an innocent man here in this very building in 1971. Not only one murder but two. You also murdered your colleague George Roberts in an effort to cover up your crime. If you had asked me if I believe in ghosts or spirits a month or two ago then about the only thing that we have in common is that my reaction might have been the same as yours.

"However, I now know different. The two men that you murdered, along with a witness, are in this very room with us now."

Clive Mellors froze in horror and looked at David, Janet, Stephen and the inspector in turn. His eyes boggled as he struggled to comprehend what he was hearing. He glared at the inspector as if he were a mad man and after a few seconds he finally spoke.

"You are completely off your trolley. You're all mad. This is a trick to catch me out. Now you're telling me that the ghost of someone called Michael Pennington and my old workmate George Mellows is coming back to haunt me? Leave it out – you're insane. What kind of a fool do you take me for?"

You could have heard a pin drop as Clive Mellors' eyes concentrated on the pencil twitching on the desk. As it rose into the air he stared in disbelief and with a chuckle of insane laughter he cowered behind his chair. He never took his eyes off the pencil, he was oblivious to anyone else in the room.

The pencil hovered against the magnolia coloured walls of the office partition. Slowly but surely the writing appeared.

Clive Mellors, my name is Jack. I watched you murder Michael Pennington. Michael is here. George is here. Your past has come back to haunt you. There is no escape.

Clive started rambling, "This isn't happening, take this away, this is illegal you have to make it stop."

There was no pity in that room and there was no let-up in the proceedings. The laptop screen glowed brightly and the words in white on a black background started to appear on the screen.

Clive, this is George. You not only killed me but you pocketed my wages after my death and went on to molest a teenage girl in flat 3 whilst you were supposed to be decorating it. I was watching you. She had a close escape didn't she? I bet you thought no one knew about that or about your fraudulent insurance claim on the van which only you and I know about. Do you want more proof? I have plenty. I have come back to haunt you for the rest of your living life. I am your worst nightmare. Welcome to the supernatural Clive!

Clive was now so distraught he was tugging at his hair and spitting and grinding his teeth in anguish. Janet, Stephen and David sat in stony silence as the drama unfolded before their eyes. No show of remorse or sympathy here. Clive Mellows was finally getting what was long overdue. It was my turn now. I had to have my say. I waited years for this opportunity. I had no remorse and no feelings for this despicable human being. No pain could compensate for what he did to me all those years long ago. I could finally vent my anger on my murderer. I was holding nothing back. I opened a word document, how I wish I could have imposed a written image, the likes of which we had just seen from George, how I longed to be able to throw something at this creep. I would have to settle for more tried and tested means. I typed my message.

Finally Clive, this is Michael Pennington. A blast from your darkest past. You now have three spirits chasing you for retribution. How do you feel about this? We will never go away. We are here forever. I can never forgive you. Welcome to hell.

That was it. After all those years and that was all I could say. The effect of all of this on Clive Mellors was actually quite disturbing. The man was physically and emotionally wrecked and his face contorted with fear and confusion. His words were incoherent as he frantically struggled with his troubled mind for an explanation.

The inspector decided to move Clive Mellors to the accountant's office. We knew it was best to stay away. We had done our work. It was now up to the inspector and the detective to secure a written statement. This was done with ease and in the presence of a solicitor who was not unjustifiably concerned as to the mental state of his client.

Taped evidence was later dutifully recorded at the police station and we heard from the inspector that Clive Mellors put up no resistance and seemed consigned to his fate. He had no interest in denying the charges and volunteered information with such precision and detail that there could be no mistaking the authenticity of his statement.

As the unhappy murderer left the office under arrest and escorted by two policemen, the inspector looked at Janet inquisitively as if to enquire as to where Jack and I were standing. Janet gestured in our direction and the inspector turned to us and addressed us.

"I am so sorry that I ever doubted you. You have to admit it was hard to believe. It has been a pleasure to work with you and I am deeply honoured to have been of assistance. As for standing in the middle of an office in Oldbury and talking to myself in such a way, I feel that I should perhaps take early retirement and enjoy life more. After all, one thing that you have taught me is that life is too short and I intend to make the best of what time I have left. As for fabricating police evidence, this shall remain our little secret. After all, no one will believe what has happened. It can hardly be proven. I wish you all the very best and I hope that you can now follow whatever destiny lies in store for you."

Without another word the inspector made a hasty exit followed by his detective who even turned towards us and said goodbye. "Nice knowing you guys," were his nervously spoken and parting words.

I had to speak to Jack and made straight for the laptop. I was totally unprepared for what came next.

Michael: Jack are you OK? We finally did it didn't we. What a result.

Jack: Michael, my dear friend. It is time for me to go. I can see a bright light and something is drawing me. I am not afraid it and it is a pleasing experience like something is calling me home. I can hear the voices of my family and friends. I don't like to leave you but I have to go. There is nothing to fear for the future, Michael. I am not departing this life by any force or undue pressure. I can remain if I wish but I feel my work is complete. I want to go. I want to move on. Goodbye Michael. I hope to see you soon, I know we will meet again. Say goodbye to Janet and the others. It's time to move on.

I suddenly felt alone. Jack had gone. Where had he gone? What of George, where was George? What was happening? At the time I could not understand why I was left without my spirit friends. I soon learned that I would have to wait until my burial before I would have the chance of moving on. There were other considerations too. I was about to make an outstanding discovery and I would be faced with a choice that was one of the most difficult decisions of my past, both as a human and a spirit.

What Happened to George?

After Jack and George left I felt quite alone and emotional despite the fact that Janet and David spent considerable time with me and constantly provided me with a source of companionship and comfort.

When I finally met Inspector Smith for the last time he was in a jovial mood and full of life and confidence. He looked much younger and at peace with himself and had resigned from the police force and taken early retirement. He could hardly contain his excitement as he told us about the misfortunes of a certain Clive Mellows. It was a harrowing tale.

Clive never stood trial. He was deemed unfit and mentally incapacitated and sectioned under the mental health act on a permanent basis. The report outlined the nature of his illness and the fact that he had become quite insane and would continually rant and rave incessantly about being haunted by a spirit called George. So that was where George went? That was what he meant when he promised to haunt Clive. It all became clear now. George would follow Clive to his grave. Only then would he consider his mission complete. It was all becoming clear to me. George had found a more suitable method of revenge than any prison sentence could possibly provide.

I gain no satisfaction from knowing this. After all this is a fate worse than death and I only hope that the end is near for Clive Mellows. The man has no future and no escape from his evil past and he has shaped his own destiny. To this day I have no idea how George managed to follow Clive and remain with him in the way that he did. After all, Clive Mellows had clearly demonstrated that he had no apparent sixth sense. I shall investigate this further and try and locate similar instances of hauntings or circumstances that might explain this unusual occurrence. For now I do not have the answers.

I prepared myself for what was to come. I spent time with Janet, Stephen and David and was in regular contact with my spirit friends on the internet. I made sure my memoirs were available on the internet for people to read. After all, everyone likes a good story, don't they?

I have found many others that possess the ability to manipulate computer screens in the way that George did. This amazing phenomena will be the way in which global communication and integration will take place between the living world and the supernatural. This will take place soon in the not too distant future. We will announce our presence and our very existence to the living world. This is beyond all comprehension of course but you already know how that first contact will take place.

I am now reaching the end of my memoirs. I continue to work with a sense of urgency and advise others as I endeavour to provide them with assistance in order that they might find their true and deserved destiny. There are many choices and options that will shape our future. My own choice is one of a personal nature and provides me with a deep and meaningful sense of satisfaction and pride as I struggle to assist others and help build the network and contribute towards the mission and the integration and understanding between the living and the afterlife.

As you surf the internet and read message forums around the globe, if you happen to come across the story of Michael Pennington or someone claiming to be a spirit or a ghost, think of me. There are many such stories and outrageous claims. Only a few will understand the full implications of the global network of the afterlife. We need your help. Please spare us a thought from time to time.

As my coffin and physical remains are carried to my final resting place I shall think of you. As the bright light calls and the path becomes clear I might consider a walk into my future and once again meet up with Jack and my long lost friends and relatives. I no longer have a fear of the unknown. In fact, I look forward to it with happiness, as the day draws ever nearer. Unfortunately I shall have to postpone that eventful day.

I shall of course defer this calling and I have decided to remain here on earth for the foreseeable future. I have more work to do. I have a contribution to make. Our mission and purpose here on earth is one of great importance.

With all my Best Wishes

Yours Truly,

Michael Pennington (Deceased)